Books by Bernice Rubens

Birds of Passage
The Elected Member
Favours
Go Tell the Lemming
Sunday Best

Published by WASHINGTON SQUARE PRESS

FAVOURS

Bernice Rubens

WASHINGTON SQUARE PRESS
PUBLISHED BY POCKET BOOKS NEW YORK

This novel is a work of fiction. Names, characters, places and incidents are either the product of the author's imagination or are used fictitiously. Any resemblance to actual events or locales or persons, living or dead, is entirely coincidental.

Favours was originally published in England under the title *A Five-Year Sentence.*

WSP

A Washington Square Press Publication of
POCKET BOOKS, a division of Simon & Schuster, Inc.
1230 Avenue of the Americas, New York, N.Y. 10020

Copyright © 1978 by Bernice Rubens, Ltd.
Cover artwork copyright © 1984 Fredericka Ribes

Published by arrangement with Summit Books
Library of Congress Catalog Card Number: 78-32086

ISBN: 0-671-50278-6

First Washington Square Press printing December, 1984

10 9 8 7 6 5 4 3 2 1

WASHINGTON SQUARE PRESS, WSP and colophon are registered trademarks of Simon & Schuster, Inc.

Printed in the U.S.A.

I

1

MISS HAWKINS LOOKED AT HER WATCH. IT WAS TWO-THIRTY. IF everything went according to schedule, she could safely reckon to be dead by six o'clock. Maybe I'll listen to the news first, she thought to herself. I won't need to bother with the weather forecast.

She checked her leavings for the hundredth time. Opening each drawer in the kitchen cabinet, she reassured herself that everything was tidy and in order. She wanted to leave a good impression. She noticed one slightly chipped cup on the dresser, and that she threw away. She had polished the silver that morning and she kept opening the cutlery drawer to admire its shine. Then once again into the bedroom. She smoothed the candlewick bedspread, picking off the odd loose thread. Her two skirts, best dress, coat and three blouses hung cellophane-covered in her wardrobe, each garment on its own metal hanger. Below, her three pairs of shoes were polished and severely in line. And neatly folded beside them, the polythene bag that would finally enshroud the fur-lined boots she was wearing for her last appearance. In each of the four drawers of the chest there were two demure lavender bags. These she placed on top of her woollies, underwear and sundries, so that they were visible. She checked that the laundry basket was empty—to be caught with dirty linen would reap a shame that would haunt her in her grave—and that her cupboard was bare. Almost bare, that is, apart from a carton of long-life milk with a promise of three months' life-expectation on its packaging, during which time she would certainly be found and it wouldn't be wasted. So too, the four tins of mackerel she'd recklessly bought in an "end of line" sale. All was in order. She was ready.

She went back to the sitting-room. On the small desk lay a white envelope. On it she had written, "The Will of Miss Jean Hawkins. To Whom It May Concern." She had no idea who on earth could be concerned with it, but it seemed the formal thing to say. She had not yet sealed the envelope. That she would do immediately prior to her final act of departure. Once again she took out the single sheet of paper and checked on her neatness and spelling. "I bequeath all my savings and belongings to the Sacred Heart Orphanage, Wiston Road, London, S.W. 6." The belongings that Miss Hawkins referred to would have lent themselves easily to cataloguing. She owned no trimmings and nothing was spare. Yet she did not itemize her estate, but for one particular, a metal medallion that hung around her neck, the sole and scarce adornment of Miss Hawkins' person. It had been found about her baby body when the authorities had delivered the blanket-bundle of her to the Orphanage. It was a military medal, and pointed to a negligent soldier-sire. This single possession, Miss Hawkins itemized, and requested in her will that it be buried with her, for her father's seed, no matter how sour, could sprout no further. She ended her testament with the declaration that she was of sound mind, and signed it, Jean Hawkins (Cashier). Witnessed by Mary Woolam (Mrs. Housewife). Miss Hawkins smiled. She liked that name. It was cuddly and responsible. With a different pen and a slant to her writing, she had invented a witness. She knew no-one to whom she could entrust such a delicate authority. For she had no friends and no family.

The latter she had never known. She had never investigated her parentage. The Orphanage where she had spent the first years of her life never encouraged that line of questioning. "We took you

8

from nothing," was their blanket response to any timid enquiry. It was what they said to all the children, and she ached to know the quality of *her* nothing, the where and the why of it. But when, after fourteen years, she was put out of the Orphanage, her curiosity as to her origins had evaporated.

She folded the sheet of paper and replaced it in the envelope. She stood up the flap so that it called itself to her attention. Not that she would have overlooked it, but the open flap was by way of an order. An order to be obeyed. At all stages in Miss Hawkins' life, other people had given orders, and she had obeyed. In the Orphanage, it was Matron, at school, her teachers, and in the factory, the foreman and later on, the management. During her life, obedience had assumed the nature of a passion. An order executed gave her an acute physical pleasure, and she would seal the flap of her last will and testament with a frisson close to orgasm. Now that she had reached retirement age, there would be no more orders, and how would she know what to do with her life if there were no one to tell her? Thus it did not occur to Miss Hawkins that there was any alternative to a simple, self-inflicted quietus.

She fingered the earth of the aspidistra plant in the window. It was moist and would safely outlive her. She checked on the bottle of pills on the bedside table. "It is dangerous to exceed the stated dose." In taking the whole bottle she would not be disobeying. She would merely be disagreeing with an opinion, and that, as a last rite, she was entitled to. She put on her hat and coat, and checked once again on each drawer and cupboard. Before she left the house, she lit the gas-fire in her bedroom. It was a rare act of extravagance for one who never in her life had indulged herself. In her death-chamber, she could dare to luxuriate. She shut the bedroom door and left the house for the factory for the last time.

2

MOST OF THE FOUR HUNDRED EMPLOYEES WERE ASSEMBLED IN the workers' canteen. The tables had been removed, and the tea and coffee counter now served as a table for the business of the meeting. Miss Hawkins sat clench-fisted behind the table, and viewed the sea of faces, all of them so achingly familiar, yet each single one a stranger. She shivered and the audience thought that she was nervous and that was as it should be, for how often in her uneventful life had poor Miss Hawkins been in such limelight?

Forty-six years of devoted service to "For Your Pleasure" confectionary company had earned her this parting ceremony, this "small token of our esteem" lying gift-wrapped on the table, this "no words can express" speech that Jim Connell was at this moment delivering in words and phrases that he had hitherto declared inexpressible. Miss Hawkins glanced sideways at the notes he fingered on the table: "Has given of her cervises jenerusly," she read, and she was appalled that he'd attained the rank of shop steward with such spelling. "For forty-six years," he droned on, threatening to itemize every single day of them, "she has been a steadfast and loyal colleague." Miss Hawkins heard herself spelling the words on his poor, illiterate behalf.

She looked at the package on the table. It was indeed a "small token,'' measuring at most six inches square, with a depth, allowing for the wrapping, of about four inches. One hundred and forty-four cubic inches, she worked out. Whatever it was, she was not going to open it. She had it in mind to throw it away on her way home, gift-wrapped and all, so that she need never know that, with their gift, they had given her a reason to live beyond this day.

She listened as Jim Connell bumbled on about her long and devoted service and her first green years at the factory. She remembered the day she'd left the Orphanage. Matron had put her to work at the sweet factory at the end of the Orphanage road. The Orphanage and the factory dated from the same year, as if by arrangement the one should feed the other, and the progress from foundling to fudge-wrapper was as natural as the night that followed day. From wrapping, Miss Hawkins had graduated to the boiled sweet department, then swiftly through marsh-mallows and fondants to the factory speciality on the top floor. Chocolate liqueurs. She could go no further. At this point of promotion, most of the orphan employees, cured for life of a sweet addiction, pimpled and puppy-fatted, would seek employment elsewhere. But the management had noted Miss Hawkins' diligence and devotion to duty, and they put her in the office and groomed her as book-keeper. In her thirtieth year she had attained the rank of head cashier, a post she retained to this day.

"We owe a great deal to Miss Hawkins," the shop steward waffled on, and she wondered, but with little curiosity, how they had inscribed the gift. Though she had worked at the factory for so many years, she was pretty sure that nobody amongst the personnel knew her Christian name. "Thank you, Miss Hawkins," had been the Friday acknowledgement of four hundred wage packets. Or, "A cup of tea, Miss Hawkins?" "Have a nice week-end, Miss Hawkins," as if Miss were her Christian name. Few people in her life had ever called her Jean. At the Orphanage she had answered to Hawkins as others did to Davies, Woods or Murphy. Did whatever was inside that gift-wrapped package bear any inscribed evidence as to whom it might belong? Not just any old Miss, not just any old

Hawkins, but some indication that she was a little more than the sum of both parts.

"She worked her way from sweet wrapper to head cashier," Mr. Connell was marvelling. Yes, she thought, she'd done her best. In her small way she'd been a success, and God would forgive her for what she was going to do and square the misgivings of the Sacred Heart Orphanage should her origins be subsequently disclosed. She found herself thinking again of her childhood, as if in rehearsal of a pre-death flashback.

If anyone were to bother at any time to write the biography of Miss Jean Hawkins, who was hardly the matter of research or commemoration, they would have fastened on to her twelfth birthday as being a key to the subsequent turnings in her life. On that day two events occurred which were the stuff of which nightmares are made.

Birthdays were not over-celebrated at the Orphanage, partly because the exact date of the child's birth was often not known. So one tea-time of each month was given over to celebrations for those children whose birth was gauged within those four weeks. Matron would give each birthday child a candle, pink for a girl and blue for a boy—the Orphanage was not unmindful of ritual—which was placed in a large communal cake. The candles were never lit, both as a fire precaution and for economy's sake. Hawkins held her pink candle, mourning the white and virgin wick, and a sudden violent thought assailed her. One day, when she was rich enough to buy matches, she would set fire to the Orphanage. She would do it on a Sunday when all the children were in church, when only Matron was at home. And the children would come back and watch the fire, their faces aglow in a million candlelights. She gripped her dry candle with her small clenched fist, and she felt a trickle, slow and warm, travelling down the inside of her thigh. She crossed her legs and put up her candle hand. "I've got to go, miss," she said, blushing with the shame of her grossly ill-timed but natural calling, and she rushed from the room to the nearest cloak-room. Then she wondered why she was running. She didn't want to go at all. Yet her leg was wet, and trickling now, and threateningly close to her white Sunday socks. Matron would kill her. She leaned against the unlockable door, and looking down, she saw a thin line of blood dribble over her calf. She stiffened with fear, staring at it, willing it not to reach the sock. "Oh, God," she whimpered, and made the automatic gesture of kneeling. But fearing the blood would stain the floor, she rose quickly. It was Matron's wrath she feared most of all. "I want to die, God. Right now," she said, seeing that as her only solution. "I didn't mean it about the fire. Honestly, God, I didn't. I was only joking." God had punished her evil thoughts with blood, and Matron would find out and she'd want to discover what terrible thought God had found so offensive. "I want to die," she said again decisively, and then, to underline the seriousness of her plea, she knelt on the cold floor. "Bugger the lino," she shouted. "I want to die, God. I really do."

"Hawkins." Matron's shrill voice echoed down the corridor. Each lavatory visit was Matron-timed. Too long a time spent in such privacy indicated reasons other than the simple call of nature. A quick smoke perhaps for the older boys, or worse, experiments in self-abuse or, most healthy of all, straight-forward constipation. Any of these reasons called for attention, and Matron was ever on hand.

"Hawkins," she shouted, pushing open the door. She looked at the sobbing hulk with impatience and pulled her up from the floor, noting the blood on the lino and the red smudge on the sock. "Look at your mess," she said. And then, lifting the serge Sunday pinny, "I thought as much," she said after a cursory examination. "Wait here, young woman. I'll get you your rags."

Hawkins leaned against the towel rail, trembling with confusion. Matron hadn't killed her. She hadn't even been very angry. And what were the rags she was bringing? Was she going to be dressed in rags for punishment? But what resounded most in Hawkins' ear was the order of, "Wait here, young woman." When Matron was angry, she often said "young lady," and if she called you that, you knew it was bed without supper or no pudding on a Sunday. But "woman" was different. It was a word that belonged to old people, and she began to cry again because she was too young to be old. She heard Matron's sensible heels down the corridor. She wished she could stop her tears.

"Now stop blubbing," Matron said, not too gruffly. "It happens to us all."

"What happens?" Hawkins whimpered.

"This," she said, pointing to the blot of blood on the lino.

Hawkins wondered what she was talking about, but she was too afraid to ask.

"Here," Matron said, holding out two wide strips of cloth. "These are your rags. Two is enough," she said. "Every night before bed, you go into the staff bathroom and wash them. The staff bathroom, mind you. Nowhere else. When it stops, you come and tell me. And you must tell me when it starts again. I've got to keep count, you see, in case anything worse happens."

"Like what?" Hawkins was terrified.

"You'll see," Matron said threateningly, and she was gone, unwilling and certainly unable to clarify further.

Hawkins looked at the rags. Her name, in black marking ink, was inscribed lengthwise on the cloth. It happens to everybody, Matron had said, but by some natural instinct Hawkins knew that boys didn't have to wear rags. But whatever Matron had said, there was no doubt in Hawkins' mind that the blood was a punishment from God. Its timing could not be ignored. Later on that day, when Matron forbade Sunday baths to Morris, Davies, Downes and Hawkins, she wondered for what morbid sin they, too, had been punished, and like a reluctant leper, she joined the rag-girl community.

The second event that was to terrorize Hawkins' future, she had desperately but clumsily buried in her soul. It took place later that same night when everybody was in bed. Hawkins woke suddenly, remembering that she hadn't washed her rag and that she was in no position to avail herself to further punishment either from God or from Matron. Quietly she crept out of bed. On her way to the door, she wondered why Morris's bed was empty. Silently she tip-toed across the landing to the staff bathroom. The door was closed but there was no light from the crack beneath. She turned the handle quietly, and in the silence, she heard the rain drumming on the bathroom window. It frightened her, as if its beating would telegraph across the entire Orphanage the news of her gross negligence. For a while she hovered in the darkness, fighting back her tears and her fear, then her hand trembled towards the light switch.

Spot-lit by the naked bulb, Morris hung from the ceiling. The tongue lolled out of her mouth, and the big toe on one small white foot was upturned in a rigid and offended cramp. Around her young neck was tied a reef-knotted necklace of damp rags, each indelible, leprous name coupled with another. Oh, Matron will be ever so cross, Hawkins thought, and she wondered what was Morris's first name. She clasped her hands over her mouth, vainly stifling a scream. Then she was sick and sobbing, and the bathroom was full of people and smells and sighs and horror. Somebody stuffed something into her mouth, and in the morning when she woke up, Matron was standing by the bed, telling her over and over again that she'd had a bad dream. "A terrible dream, dear."

"Yes, yes," Hawkins was happy to agree. "It was a nightmare."

And she got up and went about her orphan-woman's business, trying not to notice that Morris wasn't there.

Miss Hawkins stared out at the crowded assembly and shivered. She glanced again at Jim Connell's ill-spelled memorandum which no longer bore any relation to what he was saying. By his droning repetition, he seemed to be running out of expressions, and she was grateful that it would soon be over.

"And on behalf of the staff and management, I would like to present you with this gift as a small token of our appreciation."

He was handing it to her. She half stood up to accept it, her hands trembling. She thought of Morris again. I never really cried for her, I must mourn her, she decided, before I go. The tears were already pricking behind her eyes. She sniffed audibly and the audience saw her trembling. They whispered amongst themselves that she was overcome and they were embarrassed, and the more human amongst them hated her for the guilt she bred in them.

"Open it, Miss Hawkins," someone shouted from the back of the hall. She pretended not to hear. But the shout came again, louder this time, and it was an order. And she, who all her life had obeyed, began clumsily to untie the silver knot beneath the plastic instant bow. Her hands trembled so that she was incapable of untying it, and with great fury she tore the ribbon apart, tearing at the paper, hating them all for their pitying charity. She was like a ravenous dog with a bone, and the audience shifted uncomfortably, deciding that it was probably the first present poor Miss Hawkins had received in her whole life. Then they regretted the ungenerosity of the gift they had given her.

At last, she'd stripped the package. It was a book. She'd guessed that by its shape as she tore the last lining of tissue. But not an ordinary book. For it was fastened with a gold Gothic lock with two small keys attached. On its green leather binding was inscribed, MISS HAWKINS' FIVE-YEAR DIARY. She stared at it, somehow gratified that the apostrophe was in the right place. Then her knees buckled and she had to sit, gripping the edge of the table as if it were the rail of a dock. As if they had passed their verdict on her forty-six years of service. A gilt-edged, inscribed, five-year sentence. Anything, she whispered to herself, anything on earth would have been better. With total obedience, a book would have detained her no more than a week. A simple bar of soap, with diligent bathing, would have held her for less than a month. But a five-year sentence took five years to serve. No more, no less. She fingered the golden keys. Lockable too. From whom should she hide it, and for what purpose? What secrets, dark and beautiful, could it ever hold?

"Speech, speech." That same insistent voice came from the back of the hall. She wondered when, if ever, the vultures would be satisfied. She gripped the table and raised herself, digging her heels into the carpet. "Thank you," she spluttered, "it's exactly what I wanted."

FAVOURS

As soon as she reached home, Miss Hawkins turned out the gas-fire in her bedroom. For a while she sat in the room, holding on to its warmth and the shadow of death's embrace that obedience had denied her.

Five years. It was the longest and the most unjust order she had ever been given.

3

DURING THE FIRST WEEK OF MISS HAWKINS' SENTENCE, THE entries in her diary read as follows: "Monday. Got up 8:30 A.M. Washed, dressed, had breakfast. 1 P.M. had lunch. 4 P.M. had tea. 7 P.M. had supper. Went to bed 8:30 P.M. Nothing happened."

Tuesday's entry was exactly the same, and so was Wednesday's, except that the meal-times were omitted. But every day "nothing happened." The following week was blank but for the Monday when she had merely recorded getting up. Thereafter the pages were empty as if even the appetite to inscribe "nothing happened" had deserted her. In fact, after the first week of her retirement, Miss Hawkins had stayed largely in bed as a simple solution to day-swallowing. But on the sixth day, the primal needs of hunger drove her out to view the empty bread-bin and jampot. It was a moment of decision. One way of dying was not to eat, and one way of fasting was not to buy food. It would be a slow and painful demise, but not slow enough to span the five blackmailing years her former colleagues had given her. The diary lay locked on the kitchen table. She opened it resignedly and flicked through the empty week that the bed had swallowed and the almost two thousand pages that had somehow to be converted into eventful vocabulary. Her stomach rumbled, and picking up a pencil, she scrawled angrily across the current page, "Went to buy food," and quickly she dressed and went out to obey the diary's order.

As she shopped, sparingly now, because she was mindful of her reduced income, she was surprised at her sudden feeling of well-being, and she remarked to herself on her sprightly step. She paused at the bacon counter to try and analyse this sudden change of heart, and falteringly she ascribed it to the diary's command. She was obeying and that was just like being at work. She had retired from her colleagues, from a nine-to-five discipline, from a regular canteen three-courser, from the punctual elevenses, but above all she had retired from obedience, and it was that that she regretted and missed most of all.

"Oh, what fun," she said to the bacon, and those who passed her thought, Poor woman. She spends too much time on her own. When Miss Hawkins heard her own voice she realized that they were the first words she had spoken in over a week. She tried her voice again, and again to the bacon with which she felt a secure familiarity. "You've gone up again," she said reprovingly. Her voice squeaked as if it needed oiling. I must talk a little more, she said to herself, and she decided that thereafter she would read aloud to keep her voice in trim, just in case one day she would wish to use it for communication. It was the first time since her retirement that she had consciously envisaged a future. She was in a hurry now to go home and tick off the diary's command. She finished off her shopping, buying only as much as she needed for that day. Tomorrow and every day the diary would order her to the shops again. She began to sing softly to herself, and when she reached home, she ticked the order with a red crayon. She had obeyed, and she trembled with the thrill of subordination. It was natural, then, that she should think of giving herself daily orders, so that her diary would concern itself with her future rather than with her past which had proved so lamentably uneventful. This decision excited her, and bold now, she took the pencil and inscribed, "Went for a long walk."

She made herself a filling, if not nutritious breakfast, then took to the streets again. She had been ordered a long walk, so long it had to be. Not far from her street, there was a park, and although she'd lived in her little flat for over twenty years, she had never actually walked inside the park. On her way to work each morning, she had passed it in the bus, and the layout of the park had always intrigued her. It lay behind a small church, and because of that, half the park was taken up as cemetery. The other was a children's playground, surrounded by lawns and trees. The swings and slides stood adjacent to the graves, as close as lovers, with no concession of a rail or a fence to separate the living from the dead. Often when the bus stopped at the lights by the church, Miss Hawkins would watch the old men loitering without intent on the graveyard benches, and the mothers on their guardian seats, each with their own sense of detachment and privilege, yet the children passed between the quick and the dead without surprise. She would go to that park, she decided, and she would walk around it many times. A circular walk, but she would give it length in its passage of time.

There were two entrances, one, a locking-gate that led into the mortal ground, and the other, a free turnstile into the playground. She took the turnstile, intending her graveyard explorations to be casual. She skirted the sandpit and stood at its edge, watching two bucket-laden children building a castle. Only once had she been to the seaside, in her pre-woman days at the Orphanage. She could remember very little about that day except for her cry of astonishment when she saw the vast open sea for the first time. Matron had told her to keep her voice down and to behave like a lady. One day, she hoped her diary would order her to the seaside, and she would greet the sea with an unstrangled cry. She felt herself smiling again, and she took off her glove and outlined the unaccustomed creases on her face, and though the notion of happiness had never occurred to her as part of her birthright, she dared to wonder whether she was not entitled to it after all.

She turned and walked towards the swings. They were empty, and with her ungloved hand, she pushed one gently. She was aware that it was a gesture completely alien to her former self, and it convinced her that Hawkins from the Sacred Heart Orphanage, and Miss Hawkins from the sweet factory, were no more. She crossed over to the mothers' benches. Two women sat there, apart and un-speaking, separately observing their respective children playing in the sandpit. She hesitated at the bench. She was tired enough to sit, but she didn't want to admit of any punctuation between the swings and the graves. She didn't see herself specifically as part of either side. Though she had missed out on the joys of swings and rounda-bouts, it was never too late for first childhood, and for her, the sec-ond childhood of the other side was premature. So she passed through the unseen barrier without wonder.

An old man sat by one of the headstones. It was crumpled and its legend indecipherable. It could have had for him no kin-connexion, for by its age and layers of verdigris, it signalled a long-past century. But as a reminder of his future journey, it would serve as well as any other. With his stick he traced a circle on the gravel, round and round in ever-decreasing rings. Until he found his still centre, and there for a while, he rested, and looked up at her, but saw her not at all. A child darted past him, vaulting the grave, and in his fleet landing, disturbed the old man's sad geome-try. He sucked in his parchment dewy cheeks, and circled again with his stick. Miss Hawkins walked past him and smiled at him, though his eyes were on the ground. She passed through the play-ground again and hesitated at the slide. Had she been alone, she would have climbed the steps, and in her old and pensionable age, she would have claimed a childhood that had been denied her. One day, late at night, when children were too tired to swing, and old men too circle-giddy, her diary would send her to the playground to redeem her early years.

She circled the park and the graveyard many times, never fol-lowing the same route, reading aloud those tombs that were legi-ble, hearing her strong voice applaud the dead she'd never known. She marvelled at herself and at the feeling of warm goodwill that invaded her. She noticed how quickly she was walking, with an en-ergy that indicated that she had somewhere quite positive to go, and that there was not enough time to enjoy the small and simple pleasures that had been denied her.

When she reached home, she looked at the clock on the wall.

She had been walking for over two hours. She ticked the item in her diary. She had obeyed.

She took off her coat, and in doing so, realized that that, too, was an unusual gesture. Normally on returning home from work or shopping, she kept her overcoat on till bedtime, as if to secure herself in one mortgaged home within another. Now she threw it off her shoulders with a teenager's carelessness. She picked up the pen that lay in the leaves of her open and eager diary, and wrote, "Had lunch, then an afternoon nap. Started to read a book." She shrieked with delight at that suggestion, but the order presented some problems, for she had read most of the paperbacks on her shelf. It gave her an idea for a new order the following day. Her diary would send her to the library. Meantime she combed through the shelf for something unread or forgotten, and found it in a small book of country verse, its yellowing pages uncut. For the rest of the day she obeyed her diary to the letter, ticking off each order as soon as it was carried out, and when she went to bed that night, Miss Hawkins accepted that she had just spent the happiest day of her life.

For the next few weeks, the diary gave her orders, each carefully prescribed within the limits of possibility. Miss Hawkins ticked off window-shopping, library visits, a chiropodist and a hairdresser. The order to read was a daily one, and once she was so absorbed in a book that she forgot to look at television, though it was clearly ordered in the diary. She refrained from ticking it off, but postponed the order till the following day, and thereafter it was not regularly dictated. The assumption between the diary and Miss Hawkins was that the television was not obligatory and could be watched at will. Meals were no longer inscribed either, nor the simple facts of getting up and going to bed. Life had become too full to record such trivia. So she lived as the diary dictated to her, and the weeks passed in a warm current of pleasure she had never thought possible. But pleasure, as her recent reading of poetry had taught her, was a feeling that fell short of itself if not shared. Miss Hawkins had to admit to herself that she needed a friend. Her reading of poetry had compelled her, too, to thoughts of love, and she blushed even at the thought of it. But such a fulfilment was a total impossibility, and her wise diary would never dictate it. Yet though loving might be out of the question, companionship was a less remote practicality. And as she sat one evening eating her supper, the table laid with meticulous care, she set herself to thinking about the odds on friendship. Directly opposite her, on the fireplace wall, hung an oval mirror, and as she watched herself eating, she hit upon an idea. She was so excited that she left the table with her mouth still full, an offence that would have given Matron apoplexy. She went straightway to the cleaning cupboard and brought out a duster, together with a tin of lead polish that she used for blacking the grate. Her idea so enthralled her that she almost forgot to let the diary dictate it. And rushing back to the kitchen, she wrote in large capitals, for it was the boldest order to date, "INVITED A MAN TO DINNER." She was shocked when she saw it written down. It was only a white lie and the diary would forgive her, and she would tick it off with a pen, rather than with the customary red crayon, to show that it was an order of a different kind.

She went straight to the oval mirror on the wall. Winding the cloth tightly around her index finger, she smeared it liberally with the lead. Then, viewing the oval shape as a human face, she placed her finger where she gauged the mouth would lie, and in that space she drew a handsome handlebar moustache. She trimmed it a little, tapering off the corners to give a waxed effect, then, standing back, she viewed her work with infinite satisfaction. She put the cleaning things away and came back to the table. Then lining up her chair so that it squarely faced the mirror, she sat down and aligned her own face in the glass, so that the moustache grew on her upper lip. She smiled. She had a dinner-mate.

She stared at her companion for a long time, noting how like her he was, and how much they must have in common. A silent man, she decided, but strong.

"I'm so glad you could come," she said.

He smiled back at her before lowering his face to the plate. She was suddenly shy. She was so unpractised in contact with an individual. She had managed in the factory because the company of four hundred allowed for being alone. Now, face to face with a particular, she did not know how to arrange her features, and she kept her face well into her plate, fearful of revealing her gaucheness. She knew that her mustachioed alter ego was only a game, yet she regarded him with utter seriousness, as an understudy, as it were, for a possible reality. She opened her mouth for voice practice. "It's so nice to have company when you eat," she said, and she looked up and saw him smile in agreement. His handlebar had slipped a little, and she was quick to re-align herself, because he looked so silly with his moustache askew. She finished her meal, assuming that he didn't want a second helping, since she herself was satisfied. She stood up and thanked him for coming, and she moved away from the table and he was gone. Before going to bed that night, she entered into her diary, "It was a wonderful evening." It was the first time she'd allowed herself a personal commentary.

She didn't invite the man to supper every evening. From her reading she had learned that familiarity bred contempt. So she was sparing with him, not wishing to appear too eager. Those nights when Miss Hawkins dined alone, she removed the painted mirror from the wall and sat facing the dead oval stain it had left on the wallpaper. She had called him Maurice, not by any conscious deliberation, unaware that it was a name that clung to the fringes of her nerve-ends like a burr. One day she would tell him about Morris, and he would know that he was in some way a memorial.

Over the weeks Maurice served to whet her appetite for a real companion, and she thought perhaps her diary was ready for an order to that end. She was not wholly confident, and each day she postponed such a command, for failure to obey the diary would disturb her deeply, and her farewell present would then lose the only raison d'être that allowed her to accommodate it at all. One evening, dining with Maurice, she risked telling him about his namesake. The story of young Morris's sad and wasted life, and of her horrible and needless death, resounded against the walls without an echo of respect, and she desperately longed for feed-back. She slept badly that night, fitfully dreaming of the young swinging shadow. Poor Maurice's insensitivity had intensified her distress. She needed someone who could still her anguish. And on the following morning, daring herself to the sin of non-obedience, she wrote in her diary, "Went to the library and met a man."

4

SHE HAD ALREADY REACHED THE LIBRARY BEFORE SHE REALIZED the difficulty of the assignment the diary had set her. To engineer the conditions under which to meet a man could be a dangerous undertaking. Exciting, too, she had to admit, and a very positive change from the non-risk pursuits her diary had hitherto prescribed. She noticed how her steps faltered, as if aware of the dangers she was courting. She wondered whether a library was an opportune place for such a meeting. It's true it was public and therefore safer. But it was silent, too, a place for eye communication, the exchange of smiles, expressions of feigned bewilderment or simple curiosity. Miss Hawkins had no schooling in these subtler forms. Speech was her only weapon of contact. She thought perhaps she should go to the market-place, where there was noise in plenty, and one more greeting between strangers would hardly be noticed or judged, but the diary had specified the library, and there was no joy in ticking off a modified order that had been falsely tailored to one's own convenience. She climbed the stairs slowly, and at the top hesitated between the lending and the reference rooms. It was really a choice between a mobile or sedentary approach, and she preferred a situation which allowed for a moving off if communication failed. Besides, the silence in the reference library was faintly hallowed, having to do with serious study, and should a remark be overheard, it dared not be trivial. Whereas, "Isn't it a lovely day?" would echo very nicely along the fiction shelves. So she moved into the lending section and straight to novels. She looked sideways along the shelves, but from A to Z there was no man in sight. A few women browsed among the books, assessing the bait in the blurbs. She wandered through the maze of shelves. Things looked better in the history section, and the religious department was almost exclusively male-dominated. So she made her way in that direction and found herself facing Islam and Judaica. With feigned interest and deliberation, she extracted a book and opened it on the first page, keeping her eye the while on the browsers around her. "In the year 586 B.C.," she read, "the people of Canaan underwent a devastating experience." Miss Hawkins laughed, hoping to draw a timid attention to herself. The man alongside her looked in her direction, and she turned her grinning face and gave it to him. Unnerved, he moved away. She replaced the book. She would have to try another ploy. Alongside the history shelf was a backless bench. She took a book at random and sat down. She smiled at a passer-by, and he hurried on. She wondered what was the matter with her, why people didn't react to her offerings. She was decently dressed and her looks were passable. She could improve herself, she knew, with a little make-up, but the Orphanage had drilled into her a contempt for personal adornment as being offensive to God, and though she had long ago cared little about giving offence to that quarter, her mistrust of cosmetics had persisted. She would overcome her resistance, she decided. She would enlist unnatural aids to make herself more attractive and on the way home she would buy herself the basic cosmetic essentials. No. She would go home first and write such an order in the diary. But she knew she could not go home before obeying the instructions she had already ordered. She had to meet a man and she would stay in the library until she did. She looked about her. There were few enough eligibles and most of them were engrossed in their reading. She regretted her impulsive choice of library as a meeting place. It required too much mise-en-scène. The open air would have been more casual.

She decided to try the reference section, but as she opened the door, the solid wall of silence frightened her, and quickly she withdrew, knowing that nothing pertaining to her commission could be accomplished amongst its shelves. She stood disconsolately on top of the stairway, wondering where next to go to fulfil her duty. Then at the foot of the stairs, a man appeared, an oldish man, but spry in his gait. His head was bowed, checking each foot on the steps, and unseeing, he walked straight into Miss Hawkins' trap. She looked down on him and waited. When he was almost at the top, she herself started the descent. Seeing another pair of feet in his line of vision, the man stopped and looked up. Miss Hawkins stopped, too, and smiled at him. "Isn't it a lovely day?" she said, giving voice to the line she had rehearsed all the way to the library. He stared at her. Then, with his hand, he swept the raindrops down the front of his coat, a token of his opinion of her meteorological talent.

"Well it *was* a lovely day," she said limply. "The rain must have just started." Then he smiled at her, pitying her embarrassment. He made to walk on. Miss Hawkins didn't want to lose him. The miracle of finding him in the first place was not likely to be repeated. "Oh, I forgot a book," she said, following him back up the stairs. He seemed pretty indifferent to her company, but she insisted. "What book do *you* want?" she said.

"I'm going to borrow some for my mother." He stopped and looked at her. Then shyly, and with almost an inbuilt knowledge that he would regret it later, he said, "Perhaps you could help me choose?"

Miss Hawkins had read about love, and she'd sometimes eavesdropped on the factory girls' courting accounts. She had no more expected it to happen to her than she would be party to a lottery win, but at that moment Miss Hawkins was convinced that the tremors that tingled through her body could only be labelled love, and this recognition so astonished her that she was afraid to move her body lest the tremblings became audible.

"Would you?" he said. It was not a plea, but a mere followup of what he had said before.

She nodded her head and could not stop it nodding. The man continued the ascent, and with stiff steps she followed him. When they reached the shelves, she said, "What sort of books does your mother like?" She heard a caress in her voice, and she decided she had fallen in love with his mother, too.

"She likes thrillers," he said. "She's read most of these anyway, but if I let enough time elapse between the borrowing, she forgets she's read them before."

Though his accent was distinctly working-class, Miss Hawkins was impressed with his vocabulary. He was a man of some education, probably self-taught, and she already felt herself unworthy.

"I like thrillers myself," she said, sensing that the way to his heart was through an alignment with his mother.

"Woman's stuff," he said, and he blunted his contempt with a laugh. But contempt it was, all the same. Inside herself she agreed with him. Women were silly and of an inferior nature.

"D'you live with your mother?" she said. It was perhaps a way of asking him whether or not he was married, and she congratulated herself on the deviousness of the question.

"Yes," he said, and he was clearly not going to say any more.

"What a good son you must be."

And again he laughed and again the laugh was a cover. He picked out a book with a singularly lurid jacket. "This is the sort of thing," he said, flashing the naked, blood-dripping torso before her eyes. She shivered, more from embarrassment than horror.

"Too gory for you?" he asked.

"No," she said quickly. If it suited his mother, it had to be fit for her. "I like to frighten myself."

"Just what she says," and at that moment, Miss Hawkins saw herself well and truly married, sharing the house with the old woman, feeding her with dead bodies in closets, blood-stains on carpets, the smell of burning flesh, a million malevolent malignities that would keep her busy and out of sight and eventually out of mind.

29

"Here's another," he said. He showed her the cover. A young girl hanging from a meat-hook. She thought of Morris, or rather the thought of Morris surfaced, for it was a permanent subtenant in Miss Hawkins' mind. It was all Matron's fault, she thought, who took the money that bought the ink that marked the rags that made the string that choked the maiden all forlorn. She wondered how Matron had died, if dead she was, and hoped with fervor that her demise had been slow and infinitely painful. She felt her teeth clench with the outrage. Sooner or later she would have to share Morris with somebody. Sooner or later she would gently have to cut her down and bury her. More and more as she grew older, the ghostly image swung relentlessly in her head, to and fro with metronomic regularity, the upturned toe sheering her nerve-ends, orchestrated to the screaming apology of a young white face that had proved itself to be that of a woman. Miss Hawkins looked at her companion. "What's your name?" she said. She had to know that and she had to know it in full.

"Brian," he said. "Brian Watts. And yours?"

"Miss Hawkins." She obeyed her time-honoured conditioning.

"Miss what Hawkins?"

Out of her past she plucked that infrequent monosyllable. "Jean," she said.

He had by now gathered a half a dozen books. "I wonder if it's stopped raining," he said. He walked over to the window. She took in the full-length view of him for the first time, and she noticed that his shoes needed heeling. She ascribed it to negligence rather than poverty. How could a man who spent his life looking after his mother find time for personal attention? Soon her diary would order her to take Brian's shoes to the mender's.

He came back to the shelves. "It's pouring," he said.

She wanted to detain him, to give him some reason to shelter from the rain other than that of her own company. On her way into the library she'd noticed without interest that there was an exhibition of war pictures in the annexe. It would do. She told him about it. "We could look at that until the rain gives over." She thought of all the orders she could have given herself that morning in her diary: "Helped a man to choose books for his mother." "Went to an exhibition" and heaven knows what events would follow. So many red ticks in such an abundance of obedience. But the diary would never be that ordinary, even though there was now more than adequate copy in her life to justify a journal. Her diary was an order book, and would continue to be so if her life were to have any purpose at all. She might never see Brian Watts again. She might be alone for ever, and the single reliable joy in her life was the daily red-crayoned tick, and that pleasure she could not jeopardize.

"Alright," he said.

They descended the stairs and she waited while he checked out his mother's borrowings. The exhibition was in the annexe of the library, and they had to walk through a covered way to reach it. The narrow path was irregular with grassy humps and holes, and without thinking of the consequences, she crooked her arm so that he might lend her his for her support. And he did, because he could not leave it just jutting out into the air. At the touch of his arm, Miss Hawkins had a sudden desire to go home. She feared that her body could no longer tolerate the battering of such frequent and unaccustomed pleasure. Even though she had invited it herself, she could not believe that she was the object of anybody's attention, and she tightened her elbow on his hand as if she would keep it there for ever. She wanted its imprint indelible on her skin so that it would be proof to Maurice at dinner that this had really happened to her and that it was no mere figment of her frustrated imagination. At the end of the path she released her grip. There was a revolving door into the exhibition, and Brian hesitated. It was a contraption that he always tried to avoid because it frightened him a little. But there was no other means of entry. He wanted Miss Hawkins to go first, and to this end, he placed his hand on her shoulder, guiding her as the path-beater through the door. Miss Hawkins' body was now feverish, and she would have liked to sit a while on one of the leather settees that flanked the exhibition. But she did not want to call attention to a fatigue that might have betrayed her age, for she was suddenly conscious of that, too.

"I've a stone in my shoe," she said, marvelling at her sudden duplicity. "D'you mind waiting?"

He sat down beside her. She turned her back slightly, needing to hide the stone that wasn't there. At the end of the settee stood a large potted plant, and coating the earth was a lining of small white stones. Surreptitiously she slipped one into her hand and into her shoe as she eased it off her foot. She smiled to herself. She was discovering talents that she never thought existed, and it encouraged her to be henceforth more bold in her diary's orders. For almost everything was accomplishable. She held up her shoe and ostentatiously emptied it, catching the rolling stone and replacing it where it was found.

"I've never been to an exhibition before," she said, unashamed of this display of unworldliness.

"Not even the National Gallery?"

"Where's that?" she said.

"In Trafalgar Square."

"I'd like to go there one day."

He couldn't leave that hanging in the air. She had made an obvious request, and there was no-one else around to fulfil it, so he said, "We'll go there one day if you like."

She wanted to beg him to desist, to avail himself no more, to give her time and peace to assimilate the momentous gestures and words he had already donated. After such a long emotional fast, her lustful appetite was large only in principle. Her capacity had sorely shrunk and any overload was painful. "One day," she said.

They sat in silence, and though she was grateful for the pause, she was equally afraid that, if prolonged, she would lose him. "Shall we look at the pictures?" she said.

He got up and stood beside her. Then, in a deliberate movement, he crooked his arm, as if ordering her to take it. Out of his own weakness, and lack of self-assertion, he rarely took the initiative in any situation, but when he did, it was performed with the vicious aggression of a bully, as if he despised himself for his own weakness. "Let's get on with it," he said.

She took his arm quite naturally, as if it were her proper due, and she worried that, after a lifetime's deprivation, she could so quickly attune herself to its very opposite, and more than simply attune but actually to take it for granted. Yesterday and all her yesterdays, she had walked alone, her body-skin hard-calloused with disuse. Now suddenly it craved attention, and with wanton appetite, not simply as a plea, but as a downright expectation, peppered with anger at being so long deprived. She would have to take a strong hold on herself not to become too greedy.

They were facing a collection of factory pictures, with single close-ups or straightforward rows of girls packing munitions. She had been one of those girls, with the same white muslin turban and white overall that gave an odd look of purity to the lethal poison that shuffled between their fingers. During the war, the "For Your Pleasure" sweet factory was given over to ammunitions, and the same girls who so deftly wrapped the mints, now equally skilfully encased the bullets. She had never questioned the dubious morality of her work. For her it was simply a question of packaging. Her wage had increased considerably and it was during that time that she was able to put down a deposit on the small flat where she still lived. The manager of the factory had said she was sensible. Flats were cheap in bomb-risked London, and she was wise to risk the advantage. The other girls thought her staid and middle-aged before her time. They could all be killed tomorrow. What was the point in paying out good money for a future that one might never live to enjoy? And, in fact, some of the girls turned out to be right. Especially one, she remembered, who had particularly sneered at Miss Hawkins' husbandry. Davis it was, one of the orphan-women, who, one day, sitting alongside Miss Hawkins at the conveyor belt, fell suddenly forward, her small face too frail an obstacle to impede the belt's smooth running. But the bullets accumulated in a heap on the side of her cheek, and then over her head, before Miss Hawkins, too astounded at the crumpled vision beside her, was able to drag up the turbaned head and let the bullets pass. "Davis," she screamed into the alabaster face. In its eyes gleamed a defiant I-told-you-so look that proved that there wasn't any point in mortgages after all. "A blood clot," the factory foreman told the girls in the canteen. "Went out like a light. Couldn't have felt a thing." Miss Hawkins was angry. Not even a bomb. Not even a shrapnel splinter. Just a simple death from an unnaturally natural cause. Somehow, in wartime, it seemed an illegal way to die.

"Were you in the army?" she asked Brian as they reached the "Men in Combat" section.

"Yes. But I never saw any action. It was my mother, you see."

"How could she stop you?"

"She did. But it wasn't her fault. That's what she says anyway." He steered her away from the black and white sacrifice others had been called upon to make. "Let's sit down," he said. He obviously intended to tell her the whole story and he wished to make a recital of it. Miss Hawkins was glad of the rest and grateful that he seemed to value her confidence. "I was posted to the Far East in forty-one," he said. "A couple of days before I was due to sail, she had a heart-attack. I'm the only child, you see, and my father, well, he'd disappeared. So I got compassionate leave. She recovered but only after my regiment had sailed. Then twice more I got posted abroad and the same thing happened. She was rushed to hospital each time, so it was quite genuine. But since the end of the war, she's not had a day's illness. No, I never had a proper war," he said, and there was no attempt to hide the bitterness in his voice. "My mother saw to that."

"You should be grateful," Miss Hawkins said. She looked up at the photographs. "I wonder how many of those poor men didn't come back."

"I'd been better off," he said, almost in a whisper, and though she heard it, she sensed that it was not hers to question. It would be a conversation topic for another time, and she would order it in her diary. She was confident that she would see him again, for he had told her a story that was patently only a beginning. "The rain's stopped," she said as a sudden shaft of sunlight pierced the window.

He led her towards the door. "The old woman's incontinent," he said, and again she made no comment except a mental note to remember the word and to look it up in her little pocket dictionary.

Outside, he looked at his watch. "I must get back with the books," he said. "I come here every Friday at this time."

"So do I," she said quickly, and added, with her new-found cunning, "It's strange we haven't met before."

"Next Friday, then?" he said.

She nodded as he fumbled in the inside pocket of his coat. "Here's my card," he said. "And you'd better be here." He didn't bother to conceal the authority in his voice, and Miss Hawkins found nothing strange in his tone. The switch from weakling to bully seemed the most natural thing in the world. She held the card in her hand till they reached the end of the makeshift path, where they went their separate ways. Once out of his sight, she took out her glasses and read the print on the card. It simply gave his name and address. She'd hoped for some indication of a profession, but he was obviously a full-time mother-minder. He seemed an odd man to be carrying a visiting card, and she had an instinctive feeling that poor Brian needed so desperately to have his individuality acknowledged, even if it was only by the hand of a printer. On the way home, she read and re-read his address and repeated the word "incontinent" on every second step. Her first task on reaching home was to tick off proudly the day's order in the diary. Then she went to look up Brian's word. She was shocked by its definition, and realizing the manifest inconveniences of such a condition, she resolved there and then that it was time Mrs. Watts went into an old age home.

That night she put the mirror on the wall and had Maurice to supper. She told him of the events of the day, reliving the pleasures in the telling, and of her decision as to Mrs. Watts's future. She was glad that he was seen to agree with her. He was a good guest that evening, for she made no demands on him. He shared her excitement, and thrilled to her anticipation, and above all he confirmed that the old lady should be put away. She got up from the table. "You're right," she said, "it's the only sensible thing to do."

_____ **5** _____

THE FOLLOWING FRIDAY, MISS HAWKINS ROSE EARLY. DURING
the week her diary had sent her to the cosmetic counter at the local
supermarket and she had invested in some simple aids to beauty.
Though she had practised their application many times, and
studied their varying effects, she was still a novice in the art of self-
disguise, and that morning she removed and re-applied the pastes
and the powders many times before she was satisfied. She put on
her best dress and opened the virgin bottle of Stream of Violet
which had been her most extravagant purchase. It had a very pow-
erful smell, and she was not sure where to put it on her person. It
had been too expensive to use in rehearsal, so she deliberated long
before applying it. The logical site seemed to be on her upper lip,
so that she, if no other, could personally benefit from the "exotic
power" that the label promised. The smell was overwhelming, and
she wondered whether it was too obvious a seduction ploy. But it
was too late now to wash it off, since that would have necessitated
a renewal of make-up. She hoped that in the fresh air the smell
might lose some of its pungency, and by the time Brian caught a
whiff of it, its exotic promise might have evaporated to a mere suggestion.

It was eleven o'clock. She had noted the time of their last meeting and reckoned that Brian had ascended the library steps round about eleven-thirty. She would be there waiting for him. She was too unsure of their relationship to risk a late arrival. She went to her diary, and before filling in the day's commissions, she flicked back the pages and delighted in the red-crayoned ticks that dotted every page. Not once had there been a lapse of duty. She decided that each day she would grow more bold, for there was more joy in a tick that had been perilously earned. So she wrote, "Went to the library and met Brian," and since that order was so easily executed, she dared herself to another. And with a trembling flourish, she wrote, "I kissed him." But even she knew that as a cheat. An order that incurred her own activity was easily honourable. She had to set herself a more stringent test. So she crossed out the initial command and wrote instead, "Brian kissed me." Then, fearful of the consequences, she left the house.

She was early and there were few people in the library. She wandered along the fiction shelves, keeping one eye on the clock. By eleven-thirty she had combed the novel section, and fearful of drawing attention to her long loitering, she hid herself in the niche where the catalogues were kept. From this vantage point she had a good view of the entrance door, and there she took her stand, flipping through endless titles and subject matter until she heard the church clock strike twelve. She began to panic, less at Brian's nonappearance than at the receding possibility of ticking off the diary's order. For the first time since her retirement, she began to dislike the diary a little, to resent its impudent hold on her. Its order had been cruelly specific. It was not any man she was to meet at the library. It was Brian, and it was Brian's mouth that was ordained to land on hers. She went to the reference library and tip-toed self-consciously through the learned silence. She even tried the children's library, allowing for the possibility that his mother had, in the course of the last week, degenerated into second childhood. But nowhere was there sign of him. She went back to the fiction shelves and waited. She decided she would give him till one o'clock. She would postpone any further decision until then.

She took a small mirror out of her bag to check on her make-up.

It had clearly lost the bloom of its first application. She blotted the streaky foundation with powder and applied a new layer of lipstick. She sniffed and noted that the "stream of violets" had dried up completely, and she began to dislike Brian a little. She picked out a book at random and started to read, but she couldn't concentrate, and she read and re-read the first sentence over and over again. She was aware of a man standing beside her, shifting from foot to foot as he pretended to read a book. He shifted sideways towards her, then looking up, he said, "Would you come to the pictures with me?"

She looked at him. His face leered from its low forehead to barely perceptible chin. A slither of spit dribbled from the corner of his mouth. He held the open library book towards her, inviting her to view the postcard he'd slipped between the pages. She feared the surge of excitement that throbbed in the region of her legs. It was sinful, she knew, and the temptation to look at the postcard was overwhelming. Yet she knew she must not look at it, so she kept her eyes reluctantly on his repellent leer. Then, mindful of her diary's orders, she said, "No. You won't do at all." And she moved away quickly because she was suddenly afraid of him, and out of the library and into the street, not knowing what to do, and not daring to go home and face her first disobedience. It was now a quarter to one and it was clear to Miss Hawkins that Brian was otherwise engaged. She thought perhaps he might be ill and he had no means of letting her know of his indisposition. Then she was suddenly anxious, wanting to care for him, wanting to shield him from the constant and nagging demands of his old mother. She opened her bag and re-read the address. He lived only a short bus-ride from the library and it seemed suddenly right and proper that she should visit him and learn the cause of his non-appearance. She walked to the bus-stop and waited. It did not occur to her that an unannounced call at Brian's house might be inopportune. Foremost in her mind was her diary's commission, and anything that facilitated its execution was in order.

Romilly Road, which was where he lived, was itself on the bus route. She knew it was a long road, a local High Street, and she would have to watch closely at the numbers to gauge the right stop for 147. She noticed the supermarket spanned one large block, and its entrances started at number 53. She got up from her seat. She guessed that the next stop would be the closest. The bus pulled up outside number 93. It meant a short walk. She hurried. She did not want time for preparation. She would knock at his door and play it by ear.

But when she reached the house, she saw that a small group of people were waiting outside. And at the kerbside stood a hearse. She hesitated, but only in her step, for her train of thought from Brian's last card-giving gesture to his illness, or accident perhaps, to his ultimate demise, was unbroken, and the sight of the old woman, presumably his mother, now being led out of the house, was its sole interruption. A single hot tear stung Miss Hawkins' powdered cheek, and reminded her that she had not wept for many, many years. Poor Morris, hooked up to her orphan-womanhood, had been the dead eyewitness of her last tear. With the back of her glove she wiped it roughly from her cheek. There would be a time for grieving. Bereft as she was, the now transparent impossibility of ticking off her diary's order grieved her even more. She could rush into the house and perhaps catch sight of his face before the wood covered him, but the box was not the library that the diary had ordered. She could perhaps, too, plant a kiss on his shrunken cold lips, but such passivity was not what the day's order had in mind. There was now no hope even of a partial fulfilment. She would rub it out, remove it with ink-erasing fluid, and pretend to her dying day that it had never been there at all.

Miss Hawkins stood aside as the old woman passed her. Her supports on either side of her took her to the kerb, where she waited, tear-stained, as the coffin, borne by four men, their faces painted with manufactured sorrow, emerged from the front door. The small crowd watched it into the hearse. Then the old lady was helped into the car behind and seated between the two women who supported her. Slowly the car drew away and another pulled up at the gate. A cluster of people walked towards it, and one of them, taking Miss Hawkins as a friend and mourner, took her arm and led her into the car. Miss Hawkins mutely obeyed. The thought crossed her mind to apologize for her non-funeral attire, but since no-one seemed to notice, she did not, therefore, wish to draw attention to her incongruous clothing. She sat stiffly on the edge of the black upholstery, allowing room for those she thought more entitled by kinship to tears. But somehow she felt that of all of the mourners, no-one had loved him as she, and the tears now rolled uncontrollably down her cheeks. No-one in the car said a word. Each dwelt in his or her own abstractions which seemed from their expressions to have little to do with grief. One of them, Miss Hawkins noticed, was actually smiling to himself, and she seethed with a sudden propriety right of chief mourner, and wished to order him out of the car.

It had begun to rain, and Miss Hawkins was glad of it, for it seemed right and proper for a funeral. She remembered it was raining when Morris died. She could still hear the sound of its beating on the bathroom window-pane, as if calling fearful attention to the horror inside. Even the following day, with the bathroom Lysolled and scrubbed, the rain still beat on the pane, as if to call out a terrible secret that still hid itself there, and every day it rained for so long afterwards. Yet there had been no box in the rain, no hearse or black car in the Orphanage drive. Matron had said it was all a terrible dream, so why should she have seen a hearse or a black car? But she hadn't seen Morris either, and she knew better than to ask Matron where Morris had gone, for in her heart she felt that Matron had spirited Morris away, or eaten her perhaps, to destroy the evidence of her neglect and cruelty. And in the back of the black car, she crossed her legs furiously, rubbing knee against knee with an implacable rage, translating her soul's outrage into a negotiable physical pain. She reckoned that Matron would now be in her eighties. It was still possible that she was alive and within Miss Hawkins' joyful reach and she could clasp her hands round the starched and wrinkled neck and wring it into eternity. Her neighbour on the black upholstery, catching sight of her tear-stained face, wondered why Miss Hawkins was suddenly smiling.

The shops and houses were tailing off and the landscape was

gradually rural. Through the wind-screen, Miss Hawkins caught sight of the entrance to the cemetery on the left side of the road, and sundry heads of marble angels, their bodies obscured by a high fence. The car slowed down and turned into the open wrought-iron gates. "We're there," somebody said, and though totally super-fluous, they were the first words that had been spoken aloud. The road between the graves was serpentine, and the speed of the car adjusted accordingly. Nevertheless, the passengers were swinging from one side to another on the sudden hairpin bends, and Miss Hawkins delighted in the abrupt nudge of thigh on thigh. On one of these involuntary moves, the man next to her moved his feet fur-ther than the car's swerve warranted, and on the next turn, she boldly did likewise, so that on arrival their feet were interlocked like a lover's knot. The car stopped, and the driver rushed in turn to each passenger door. He was anxious to get out of the rain, and he snorted at each door, urging them out with his wordless irritation. Then when the car was empty, he hurried back into the driving seat and watched the mourning black turn grey with drizzle. Then when they had safely reached the open grave, he lit a cigarette and pulled out the comic he had hidden under the seat.

Miss Hawkins hovered on the perimeter of the grave. She was aware of her foot-companion, who was standing behind her. Her ankle still throbbed with the touch of his black serge turn-up. She hadn't looked at him in the car. Somehow their nether encounter precluded a facial familiarity, for it would have diluted the ano-nymity of their alliance, and thus destroyed it. She would not turn her face to look at him, but she would follow him back to the car, and on the hairpin bends on the way home, they would renew their blind connexion.

The drizzle persisted and seemed to muzzle the words of the preacher whose voice floated and sank over the heads of the small assembly, occasionally swimming into Miss Hawkins' earshot. She caught the words, "our beloved brother," "dust" and "ashes," and through the gaps of legs in front of her, she saw the coffin being lowered into the ground. Then the old woman stepped forward, supported by the same guards, and weakly shovelled a few clumps of earth onto the box. Others followed her example, and then slowly they began to disperse, making their way back to the cars. The driver, seeing their approach, hastily stubbed his cigarette and hid the comic under the seat. Then composing his face as befitted the occasion, and cursing the eternal drizzle, he got out of the car to assist his passengers. Miss Hawkins waited while the others left, till she had a full and uninterrupted view of Brian's box. She did not wonder how he had died. The manner of his demise could not affect the unavoidable disobedience of the diary's order. She was sorry that they would not meet again, but she was angry, too, that he had so inconvenienced her strict duty rota. Once again she decided to erase the order in her little book, and to rub it out into a solid belief that it had never been there at all. She turned and walked back to the car. The driver was once more huddled in his seat, but a man stood at the passenger door, holding it open for her entry. He was smiling at her and she had to look at his face, and suddenly she didn't want to sit next to him on the way home. His brazen face-flashing had implied the need of a relationship which was nowhere near what Miss Hawkins had in mind. Thus ended their brief and misunderstood affair. She sat beside him because that was the only place, but she kept her feet firmly aslant, and she gripped the black upholstery with her hands so that she could maintain her position. But even on the sharpest S bend, the man made no surreptitious move. The message of her snubbing feet had been clear.

"I could do with a nice cup of tea," one of the mourners said.

"Well, Rita'll have the kettle on, I'm sure," said another.

Miss Hawkins could have done with a cup of tea, and she hoped that she would be invited back to the house of mourning to refresh herself with the others. It was possible that a formal invitation was not necessary and that she would be included in the post-funeral arrangements as naturally and as casually as she had been first involved. She looked out of the window, and noticed how quickly the houses passed by and how different it had been on the outgoing journey, when there had been time to record the pattern of each set of net curtains, the colour of each front gate, and the growth in every garden. Within a very short time, they were lapping the edges of the High Street, and after a few traffic-light stops, the car drew up at Brian's house. This time the driver refused the drizzle, and sat firmly in his seat, convinced he'd been civil enough for one outing. The front door of the house was still open, and Miss Hawkins could see the old lady disappearing inside. Then the occupants of the second car followed, and Miss Hawkins was somehow included in their number. She was suddenly curious as to how Brian had lived, his furnishings, his family photographs, and even perhaps to talk to his mother, but at a distance, she decided, recalling the dictionary definition of Mrs. Watts's condition.

The old lady was already seated in a high-backed chair in the front parlour of the house. On each side stood her attendants. There was some resemblance between them, Miss Hawkins noticed. On their faces was the pained look of sour and guilty kin, but she was loath to enquire their identity, since it was obviously assumed by all and sundry that she was a close friend of the family. The chairs were arranged in a circle, and a tea-trolley stood in the centre. It was laden with tea-cups, but the tea was yet to be brewed. Miss Hawkins was invited to seat herself and from the growing hum of voices it seemed that conversation was now in order. Miss Hawkins was suddenly nervous. The notion of gate-crashing another's grief was faintly offensive, but how could she tell them that she, too, was entitled to tears? She was conscious that the old woman was looking at her, and out of the corner of her eye, she could see her enlisting the aid of her supporter to identify the unknown visitor. The supporter shook her head and enquired of her partner, who did likewise. Then one of them disappeared as if to investigate further. Miss Hawkins wished fervently that the tea would come. The old woman was still staring and Miss Hawkins thought that she should leave. But then, the woman's suspicions, whatever they were, would be confirmed. Besides, she was very thirsty. She would wait for a quick cup of tea and a cake—those éclairs looked delicious—and without leave-taking she would quietly slip away. The investigator was threading her way back through the small group in the parlour, and Miss Hawkins was conscious of a sudden break in conversations and she knew that accusing eyes were pretending not to look at her. She got up quickly, nodded to the old woman, and avoiding any possible cross-examination, she slipped out of the room. She walked with her head down, in the hope of obliterating all eyewitness memory. But in doing so, she was unable to see the tray of two full china tea-pots and its bearer. At that moment, needing to see her direction, she chose to raise her head, catching the corner of the tray on her forehead. She heard the crash of china about her, and saw the spluttering of hot tea-leaves on her coat. But all that was trivial in comparison to her sudden view of the tray-bearer, empty-handed now, wet and tea-less, and staring at her in total disbelief. Which was an expression she shared as she deciphered each feature of his bewildered face and knew it for Brian. Both gave voice at the same time, and both with the same question: "What are you doing here?"

"I came to your funeral," Miss Hawkins said, which explained her share of the question as well as answering his. A few women came into the hall to inspect the damage and to pick up the crockery pieces that had scattered over the lino floor. It was no place for an intimate discussion. Staring past him, Miss Hawkins noticed an old woman standing on top of the stairs. "Brian," she croaked, "what's happened?" He turned and made a step towards the stairs. Then helplessly he turned again. There were too many things for him to handle. "Please go," he said, "my mother will see you." Then seeing the disbelief on her face, he added by way of compensation, "I'll see you in the library in half an hour."

She was gone before he could change his mind, dusting the tea-leaves off her coat and with a spring in her step and with a warm glow in her heart, not so much that Brian was so patently alive, but that the little red tick in her diary was now a distinct possibility. He would certainly be at the library to meet her, and the only hurdle to the tick was the kiss. But Miss Hawkins was confident. This was surely her lucky day.

She wondered whose funeral she had attended, and who the old woman was she had mistaken for Mrs. Watts. Brian would no doubt explain everything and they would laugh together, and it would be a recurrent topic of conversation for many meetings. But the thought was soured by the memory of Brian's fear that his mother would see her. He could hardly get her out of the house quick enough. She was suddenly angry, and quite automatically and with a natural impulse that horrified her, she not only wished the old woman good and dead, but she happily saw her own hand in her undoing. And together with this thought came the accompanying recall of Matron. She noticed how rage had clenched her fists, and she had to stop by a lamp-post on the kerb and lean against it to still her fury. She was glad when the bus came for the sheer physical occupation of boarding, finding a seat and searching meticulously through the contents of her handbag for the exact fare. When that was paid, she took out her compact and made running repairs on her face. She took her time with the powdering, so that when she was finished she was only one stop from the library and she used the time to walk slowly down the bus. She was anxious not to spend one second with nothing to do, so she marked time with her feet on the platform until the bus came to a stop. Her violent thoughts had deeply disturbed her, for she sensed with fearful premonition that one day they might well leak out of her control. It would happen in a moment of idleness, she thought, when boredom would dilute the strength she would need for their containment. I must start knitting, she thought to herself. And I shall knit a scarf that shall never, never end. She made a note to order her diary to send her to the wool shop, but such an order was kids' stuff, she thought. It would have done a few months ago when the orders were timid and fulfillable. Now she had a mind only for risk, for the element of chance in each day's entry. At the same time, she realized that she could not live at risk every single day, and there must be many dry days when a viable order would come in very handy. But she decided that whatever she had in mind to do, whether of trivial or adventurous intent, her diary would so order her simply to give herself the infinite pleasure of the red tick.

She went up the library steps, which had by now assumed for her

46

a domestic familiarity. At the top she waited, and after a while felt herself idling, so she went quickly to the fiction shelves and picked out a book. She read the words, but gathered from them little understanding. Nevertheless she read on, consuming the meaningless print in desperate occupation. In this manner, she lapped four or five pages, and in the middle of a sentence replaced the book on the shelves knowing that Brian would surely arrive soon. She reached the top of the stairway in time to see his bowed and unasserting ascent to his tardy rendezvous. She suddenly found it difficult to smile, and she arranged her features to spell out a welcome. She wondered why she was not more pleased to see him. She half expected a scolding, that she had been bold enough to allow herself to be discovered by his mother, and she decided straightaway to apologize. "I'm sorry," she said, before he reached the top, and she saw him hesitate, gathering quick substitutes for his intended scolding greeting. When he arrived alongside her, she took his arm and managed a genuine smile into his face.

"I hope it wasn't embarrassing for you," she said. "Your mother, I mean."

"I said I'd never seen you in my life before," he said. He gave what he thought was a conspiratorial smile.

But Miss Hawkins wanted no part in such a plot. "Why should you hide me from her?" she said.

"You don't know my mother."

She led him back down the steps, needing time to think of what to say next, or to decide to say nothing at all. They walked down in silence. Each thought that the other owed some kind of explanation. But Brian was biding his time, or perhaps, Miss Hawkins thought, he was waiting for a lead.

"Who died?" she said.

"The man in the flat below. He was old."

She waited, but that seemed to be all he had to say. "Who was that old woman?"

"His wife. I told her I'd help with the tea."

"I'm sorry about the tea-pots," she said.

They had reached the street and she was clearly leading him.

"Shall we walk to the park?" she said. In her mind she had ticked off half the diary's order. They had undoubtedly met at the library and the tardiness of the rendezvous in no way diminished the obedience. The biggest hurdle of the kiss was to come, and she thought the park might be an appropriate setting.

"I went to your house because you weren't at the library," she said, feeling the need to clarify her behaviour. "Imagine my surprise to see a hearse outside. I just stood and looked at it, and then somebody helped me into a car." She paused. "Oh, I'm so glad it wasn't you, Brian," she said, and having established her affection, she felt bold enough to ask, "Why are you keeping me away from your mother?"

"She doesn't like me to have friends."

"But that's selfish. You can't spend all your time with her."

"She's not well," he said limply, and there was finality in his voice that brooked no further discussion. Nevertheless, the gallant Miss Hawkins pressed on. "You should put her in a home," she said.

Brian stopped, "That would be criminal," he said.

She pushed him forward. "Well, it's none of my business," she said, sensing that it was very much her business, diary business, in fact, and her little book would have to deal with it. For the moment she had to cheer him up. They passed a poster advertising a community whist drive. His head was bowed so it was unlikely that he saw it. Miss Hawkins waited a while. "D'you play cards?" she said.

"I play with my mother sometimes."

"There's a whist drive next week," she said.

"My mother never goes out."

"Can't you ever leave her?"

"Not in the evenings."

"Then I could come and see you," she said.

Her suggestion was so outrageous that he laughed aloud, and it was her cue for sulking, which, from her romantic novel reading, was a sure prelude to a lovers' quarrel and consequent make-up. At first she sulked silently, and then, fearing that he noticed no change in her, she pouted audibly, but it emerged as an apologetic grunt. "You've upset me," she said, since words were the only way to make it clear. He did not respond and she held a sulking silence till they reached the park. They were approaching a wooden bench. "Shall we sit down?" he said.

He rarely made any positive suggestion. He must be tired, she thought, and she appreciated that a sedentary position was conducive to the fulfilment of the diary's order. He dusted the seat with his gloved hand, then dusted the glove on his shoe. He waited for her to seat herself first and she chose the middle of the bench to minimize the possible distance between them. But Brian made the most of the minimum and sat himself in the corner. She continued to sulk, and Brian wondered how to mollify her. Her suggestion that she might visit him was a territorial affront and he feared it. But he was anxious to meet her again, but on some neutral ground. He suddenly remembered that he'd forgotten to return the library books. His mother would be angry, but it would give him an excuse to visit the library again. Tomorrow, perhaps. "Are you busy tomorrow?" he ventured.

The question delighted her, but she was at pains not to show it. "Can't you see I'm upset?" she said.

"I'm sorry," he said, "but what can I do?" He regretted it the moment it was put, fearing that she might make a suggestion that he was totally incapable of acting upon. Miss Hawkins saw the opening and took the plunge. "You can give me a kiss," she said.

In his rare and tepid courting experiences, Brian had a meagre repertoire, and kissing was not part of it. The act almost repelled him. He was always at pains to avoid it, for it seemed to preclude other activities which he found more enjoyable. He regarded all sexual activities as pleasurably filthy, whereas a kiss was clean and virtuous and reserved only for family. A kiss was legal, and it had no more place in a sexual encounter than a saint in a den of thieves. Still, it would have been insulting to refuse, so he screwed up his eyes and leaning over, he aimed at the presentation of Miss Hawkins' cheek. And a second prior to his movement, mindful of obedience to the letter, she had the cunning to turn her head, so that the target became her mouth. Brian's eyes were defensively shut and for him the texture between lip and cheek was indistinguishable. He leaned back on the bench and opened his eyes. Miss Hawkins was now ready to get up and go straight home and wallow in the joy of red ticking. It had, without doubt, been the most perilous order to date and splendidly she had done her duty. She got up and he followed her.

"I'm not busy tomorrow," she said.

"Well, I'll be at the library at three o'clock. Will you be there?"

"Yes," she said. Then, after a pause, "Shall we go to the pictures?"

"It's difficult to be out so long."

"Tell her you're going to the dentist," she said with sudden inspiration.

He shrugged at the ineptness of the lie, and laughed a little, baring enough of his teeth to reveal in their falseness that it had been a long time since he had needed the services of a dentist.

"Or your doctor," she added hastily.

"I'll think of something."

They had reached the bus-stop and Miss Hawkins was anxious to get home.

"She'd have a blue fit if she knew."

"She sounds a right old dragon," Miss Hawkins said, and added quickly, "A fairy-tale dragon, I mean."

"She's alright," he said defensively. "She's had a rough time."

Miss Hawkins was glad to see his bus in the distance. She was in no mood to argue his mother's virtues. She hated her, however much Brian chose to defend her. She saw her as an incontinent obstacle to the title of Mrs. Jean Watts, and she felt her fists clenching as she day-dreamed herself to the old woman's funeral.

She saw Brian onto the bus, and when he wasn't looking, she blew him a kiss. She decided to walk home slowly, savouring the anticipation of the red tick. She re-capped on each stage of her day. The fearful rejection at the library now seemed years ago, and the wrong number funeral was like a dream and the smashed tea-pot a sudden awakening. She wondered how many other people had passed such an eventful day, and she concluded that she was a very lucky woman indeed.

She took off her coat as soon as she was indoors, and went straight to her dressing-table to comb her hair and to re-apply her make-up. The red tick on this day deserved some ceremony and she intended to look her best for the occasion. She lit the gas-fire in the sitting-room and brought the diary from the kitchen. She laid it open on the coffee-table, the small red crayon in its fold. She replaced the oval mirror on the wall so that Maurice should bear witness to her triumph. She would have him to supper that evening, she decided, and she would tell him in detail all about her day. She took the book in her lap and the crayon in one hand and she read the day's order aloud: "Went to the library and met Brian. Brian kissed me." She considered that each order had turned out to be equally difficult to fulfil and therefore deserved more than a blanket credit. She would give each order a tick to itself. She wet the red lead of the pencil and with infinite care she awarded herself a double credit. She leaned back in the chair, exhausted. She closed her eyes, revelling in the afterglow of achievement. She wondered what order she would set herself for the following day. Perhaps, after her exertions, she should now give herself some time to consolidate her position, and that in the morning the diary should order her to the safe assignments of the wool shop, library and cinema. She would put her proposal to Maurice, she thought, for he tended to agree with everything. Tomorrow she would have an easy day and allow herself to enjoy it without fear of disobedience. She closed the book and held it lovingly against her cheek. It was her life-line. It made everything possible, as today's precarious events had clearly shown. It had a life of its own. Of that she was sure. That accounted for its excitement, the utter unpredictability of where it would send her, and on what mission. It was her benevolent and sometimes tyrannous master, and she regarded it as separate from herself as the mustachioed witness on the wall. She was a woman who now dwelt in company, and she wondered how she had managed for so long to live alone.

6

MAURICE ADVISED HER TO PLAY IT COOL, AND THE NEXT DAY THE diary set the lenient orders she had expected. But she would miss the risk, even a slight one. So she wrote, "Enjoyed myself." It was hardly a challenge, but it introduced a small element of uncertainty which she had now begun to need as a stimulant to her day.

She left the house early, having taken Maurice off the wall, for she knew that that evening she would want to dine alone. At the wool shop she was overwhelmed at the prodigious range of colours and patterns. She was not a good knitter. She knew the basic rules of purl and plain, for those she had learned at the Orphanage. For some reason she considered the plain knitting stitch as virtuous, and the purl as sinful. Matron had taught that the right side of the garment was plain and purl, the wrong, and Hawkins became a victim of semantic confusion. She decided that she would knit the scarf in plain stitch so that it would be right on both sides. It had to be a virtuous pursuit, since the whole point of knitting at all was to stave off the occasional onslaughts of violence that clenched her fists and jaw. A scarf was an obvious choice, because unlike any other garment it was not necessarily terminable. It could be as long as eternity. She chose a large assortment of rainbow colours in thin ply wool and a narrow pair of knitting needles so that its growth would be slow and leisurely to offset the frenzied tempo of her fury. She was anxious now to get home and to cast on her stitches, but she remembered that knitting was reserved for therapy, and should not be indulged in for pure enjoyment, since any pleasure in its making would blunt it of its purpose. She knew she had only to think of Matron to get her fists nicely clenched, and this she decided to do on her way home.

Some events in her Orphanage life remained close to the surface, and these she could deal with without pain. They belonged to the period of Matron's holidays when she was said to be up north with her mother. At these times Miss Weeks took over, and she was fat and jolly and never wore a uniform. She dispensed with the daily inspection of ears and necks, and the rigid going-to-bed rules were bent during her week in charge. The dormitories were left to gather dust on the shelves and the unmade beds, and the washing-up piled high in the kitchen sink. On the day before Matron's return, Miss Weeks would enlist all the children into a minor spring-clean, both of the house and of themselves, and Matron returned to find all as she had left. Miss Weeks would never send Miss Hawkins a-knitting, but there were enough Matron memories to purl and plain away a lifetime.

Once a strange grown-up couple came to the Orphanage, and all the girls were lined up for inspection. "Only the girls," Matron barked, as some little boy tried to sneak into the line in the hope of a break from the monotony of his daily routine.

"It's always the girls," one brave little boy dared to complain.

"Nobody wants naughty little boys to live with them," Matron said. Then it was brightly clear to the scrubbed female line-up that one of them, one lucky one, would escape from Matron for ever. One little girl, Brownjohn was her name, Miss Hawkins suddenly recalled, an acned child, who received far more than her share of Matron's rebuff and hostility, rushed forward in desperation and clutched the strange woman's coat. "Have me," she pleaded, her acne leaking. "I'm nice, really I am."

Matron laughed at the utter impossibility of anyone on earth desiring such a child, and guided her gently, for the small public's sake, into a group of little boys. The child was clearly not in the running. The couple had scanned the line-up at a distance, and Hawkins felt the woman's eyes rest on her. Her heart pounded with the possibility of escape, and she shut her eyes, praying that the choice would fall on her. Then she felt a hand on her shoulder. She opened her eyes. The woman smiled at her and the man who was with her nodded his head. "Not that one," Matron said, loud enough for everybody to hear, "she's a wetter." The woman dropped her hand from Hawkins' shoulder and moved along the line. Hawkins opened her mouth to protest that she was dry, that never, never in her Orphanage life had she wet the bed, but her mouth was dry with hate and fear, and now in any case it was too late, because the ginger-headed Stewart passed in front of her, flanked by her new foster-parents on her trembling way to freedom. Later that day, when Hawkins was helping the maids with the washing-up, Matron came into the kitchen and gave her one of her rare smiles. "Can't afford to lose you, can I, dear? You're the best domestic in the house." She was drying a large dish at the time, and in small reply, she dropped it and watched the flowered china pieces scatter over the stone floor. And when the noise had subsided, she took a pile of plates that she had already dried, and staggering under their weight, she lifted them off the draining board and sent them to join the scattered remains on the floor. The clatter was tremendous, and she was looking around for further avenues of destruction as a way of invaliding herself out of that prison when Matron struck her across the face, and grabbed the apron bow at the back of her waist, propelling her through the kitchen and up the stairs to the end of the corridor and the single isolation punishment room. "It's bread and water for you, my girl," Matron shouted. And that's how it was, Hawkins remembered, for two stomach-rumbling days, and no sight of another creature save the stiff and conquering form of Matron as she dispensed the daily ration.

By the time Miss Hawkins reached home, her fists were tight and white with fury, and even before ticking off the wool buying order in her diary, she had cast on a hundred stitches, each single thrust of the needle a well-aimed stab in Matron's stubborn heart.

She knitted until she cooled, then she ticked off the wool shop in her diary. When she left for the library, she hesitated at the door. "Good-bye Maurice," she called, and as she walked up the street, she understood how pleasing it would be to leave somebody behind in the house, someone to whom one could, with greeting, return. To know that in one's absence some object may have been moved on a mantelpiece, some book may have been taken from a shelf, some shape, other than her own, had acquainted itself with the uncut moquette of the settee, and she resolved that her home would soon be Brian's as well.

He was waiting for her outside the library, and they ascended the steps arm in arm. She offered to return the books for him at the desk, while he went to the shelves to make his weekly choice. She watched him from a distance and noted how he collected books at random without even a glance inside. The luridity of the covers seemed to be his only guide. From the back he looked younger than his years, which she put in the mid-sixties. His mackintosh was brown and belted, and probably buckled in the last hole, since it hung loose and draped about his thighs. A small grandchild might have grabbed it as a lead, unperturbed by the huge indifference of the brown and slightly stooped back. For there was an overall unawareness about him, an isolation, as he stood there, uncomfortable at the shelves, impatient to collect his mother's quota. He turned suddenly, the six gory titles under his arm. He looked irritated but managed a smile when he caught her watching him.

"Well, that's your good deed for the day," she said, hoping that license was now given to be as sinful as he pleased.

"I hope she hasn't already read them," he said.

"She'll never notice."

"You don't know my mother," he said, and there was no concealing the anger in his voice. If his mother were to be slandered, it was only he who had the right to malign her and he resented any stranger's invasion into his private battlefield. Miss Hawkins sensed she'd made a bloomer and she hastened to take his arm as her only known means of making amends.

"You said it yourself. The other day," she said.

And because she was right, he resented it even more. She squeezed his arm and wished she knew more about the subtleties of courtship.

They were approaching the cinema. She wondered whether she ought to make a show of paying for her ticket. She knew it was the man's job to do the paying, but she did not have the confidence to see herself as part of a pair. His paying for her would confirm a relationship, his role as protector, and perhaps it was too soon to expect a commitment from him. So in order to avoid a possible disappointment, she began to rummage in her purse. They made for the ticket box and joined the line. He placed himself in front of her and Miss Hawkins saw that as a very hopeful move. When his turn came he turned to her. "D'you like to sit upstairs or down?" he said. Upstairs was posher, she knew, and far more expensive, and not knowing what her share of it would be, she hesitated. Then, "Upstairs," she risked. She heard him as he instructed the cashier. "One circle seat," he said. He took out a small leather purse and counted out the exact change, while Miss Hawkins fumbled frantically in her bag, hoping she had enough. As she counted out her change, he stood and watched her, and even when she found herself a few pennies short, he made no move to assist her. Sadly she withdrew a five-pound note from her wallet that she was loath to break into for a few more pennies. She counted out her change and followed him into the darkness. A torch guided them down the circle flight of stairs, and as she groped for her seat, she remembered her diary's order: "Enjoyed myself." She sat down and took honest stock. No, I'm not enjoying myself, she thought. She tried to ascribe his lack of courtesy to an unwillingness to commit himself, an unreadiness to play the role of consort. Yet the thought niggled her that he was just plain downright mean, and she wished she'd had more man-experience to understand whether stinginess in men was a norm. She was angry. The act of breaking into a five-pound note was always depressing, but it pained her less if it were for a largish sum, at the supermarket, for instance, for a week's shopping. To break it down for the sake of a few pennies seemed an extra extravagance, and she regretted that she hadn't opted for the stalls. She looked sideways at him and he smiled at her, then out of the blue he took her hand and instantly she forgave him. He squeezed her fingers, but such sudden ardour made her suspicious. Perhaps, she thought, he was celebrating the discovery of a companion who could pay her own way. Am I enjoying myself? she thought. She longed wistfully for a red tick, but she could not in all honesty feel that it was yet merited. She relaxed her hand in his, and decided to test him to another chance. "Shall we have tea in a café afterwards?" she asked.

He nodded, his eyes on the picture. She would give him a chance to pick up the bill, and if he paid, she could sincerely tick off the diary's order. If not—she postponed thinking of that alternative and decided at least to enjoy the picture.

It was called *The Splendours of the Night,* and the titles were just creeping up on the screen. It was years since Miss Hawkins had been to the pictures. Since her acquisition of a television set, she had seen no reason to duplicate her pleasure and pay for it in the bargain, and she tried not to think of the broken five-pound note again.

The film now seemed to have started in earnest, for at least five minutes had passed without a printed credit. They were in a ballroom. There was old-fashioned dance music, and beautiful fancy dress, and immediately Miss Hawkins was swept into the romance and glamour of the occasion, oblivious of the man at her side. So oblivious, that she didn't notice that he let loose her hand, for he, too, was transported into the unknown, longed-for country, and for each of them, the other had no possible part of it, for their fantasy was so extreme it could only contain themselves. Thus, side by side, they were separately transported into a beat of life that was never ugly, never lonely, never poor and never sick. Miss Hawkins picked on the central figure of a beautiful girl with whom to identify, and with her she would stay throughout the picture. At her side, Brian, too, was fixing on his dream-image and on a far less obvious target. His focus was the grandfather of that same young beauty, whose youth now throbbed vicariously at his side. The old man sat both at the summit and centre of his lineage, attended with

equal fervour by his peers and his inheritors. The young nurtured
and sated his carnal appetites; a single movement of a finger was
enough to conscript an army to fulfil his smallest wish. And on
every level, large or small, this continuous and loving service was
prompted above all by respect. Brian sighed. Yes, that was his
final thrust of joy. Respect, that acknowledgement that all his life
he had constantly sought and had constantly eluded him. He
blamed his mother for it, as he blamed her for everything. He had
tried to understand her. Often enough he had dwelt on her past mis-
eries, how his father had left them both, and penniless, and not a
word from the brute since he had disappeared. Daily she cursed
him and all his kind, and as she looked at Brian in his rompers, or
school-uniform, or even later in his army uniform, she heartily
wished he was a girl. But since he'd turned out like his father, then,
as a man, she would use him. And gradually over the years, she
made of him her surrogate husband and punished him as she would
have done his prototype, had he been around. All this Brian understood in hindsight, but understanding did little to increase his tolerance or to diminish the bitterness of his feelings towards her. What
worried him most was that he himself had been party to her practices, that it took two to do almost everything, including her own
brand of colonization. He bit his lips in anger, as he recalled his
years of positive submission, and at that moment he resolved that
when he got home there would be an end to it. That he would look
after her only if she begged, and only if he had nothing better to do.
Then slowly he would reverse the roles that she had insisted on.
But suddenly he remembered, too, that often in his life he had
made that decision, but somehow, in the end, she had overcome.
So he sat there gritting his false teeth with hatred, while on the
screen a young man was ushered into his presence, bowing and
scraping his way into his affection.

Miss Hawkins saw in the young man her suitor, and as he was
asking the old man for her hand, Brian was demanding a little more
reverence before granting it. Which the suitor gave and now on
bended knee. But still the old man withheld his permit and Miss
Hawkins curled her lip in disgust, convinced that the old lecher

wanted her for himself. He was to come back in a year, the old man said, having fulfilled some impossible mission, the attempt at which would most likely entail his death. "Mean old thing," Miss Hawkins whispered to her companion as the scene changed on the screen and there was an interval to day-dreaming.

"Serves him right," Brian said, still in the ebb of his fantasy. For Brian was relishing the aftertaste of power. "I don't think I want to go to a café afterwards," he said, feeling a sudden need for self-assertion. But he could be persuaded, he knew. But only if she said "please" often enough, to the extent of begging, or even buying his favours, and he would be content. It was a negative form of self-assertion, but at least it was a beginning.

"Oh, please," she said. "I do like a cup of tea. With a cream cake as well."

"I don't like cakes."

"What do you like then?"

"I like something savoury. Welsh rarebit, or mushrooms on toast."

"We can have that then."

"I can do without it," he said.

"Please," Miss Hawkins said, "I was so looking forward."

"It'll be costly," he said.

"I'll treat you," Miss Hawkins almost shouted, and regretted it as soon as it was out, recalling the order in her diary to enjoy herself.

"I'll think about it," he said, having already made up his mind.

She writhed at his side, deserting her image on the screen, while she scratched in her mind, searching for any advantage in the situation. He wanted her as his slave, she decided. He wanted her for her service. The role was not unappealing. Since her retirement it was her diary that had held her in thrall, an inanimate monitor of her obedience. Brian would simply be a human one. Yes, she decided, she could serve a double master. She had found a happy rationale for paying for his tea and subsequently, perhaps, for all his pleasures. It was prostitution in reverse, and it thrilled her with disgust and pleasurable anticipation. She made a quick reckoning of her income, assessing how much she could put aside for his sundry weekly pleasures. Bus-fares, cafés and pictures were assessable, but she had no notion of the going rates for his other little pleasures, and they were hardly a commodity that lent itself to window-shopping or price comparison. But it excited her none the less. Now the notion of being taken out and of being paid for at every turn faintly displeased her. She concluded that there was a far greater power in paying than in being paid. But Brian had fashioned his own rationale, and his conclusions, likewise dictated by his needs, were exactly the opposite.

Miss Hawkins turned her attention back to the screen and Brian likewise, and both wallowed in their separate myths till the end of the picture.

It was Brian who chose the café, one that was nearest to the style of *The Splendours of the Night* as the present century would allow. It was a large tea-room, upholstered in red plush and walled with flock. In the centre of the salon was a small fountain gushing from a fish mouth. And at the far end, flanked by potted plants, was a small gypsy orchestra who were tip-toeing through the tulips as they were ushered to their table. Miss Hawkins had never seen the like before and she wondered whether it was the first time for Brian too. She wondered how much this pleasure of his would cost her. Certainly more than the Copper Kettle she had had in mind. But power increased in ratio to the investment, so she tried not to mind his choice of venue. She reckoned she had almost five pounds in her purse, which would surely be adequate. The rest of the week she would have to economize, especially since she had already spent an unbudgeted sum on her knitting materials. The cost of survival was inflationary. She made do on her pension, but she had a little put aside over the years in a bank deposit. She would never draw on that except in the greatest emergency. She looked upon her present spending as an investment in marriage, and hopefully Brian would succumb before the nest-egg need be cracked.

The waiter handed them each a menu. It was a large coloured folder, decorated with yellow roses, which motif translated the name of the café. There was a large choice of items catering for every range of appetite, and the prices were astronomical. In a central rose-ringed box was a menu for a standard tea, which included Welsh rarebit for an optional extra of 6op. On a quick reckoning, it seemed to Miss Hawkins that it would be over-all cheaper than choosing separate items on the à la carte list, and she was quick to point out to Brian that his rarebit was on the menu.

"Yes," he said, he'd have that, and she could have his cream cake. Every large take required a little give, he decided. Thus he could prolong their unequal partnership.

A few couples were dancing round the fountain, and the bandleader moved among the tables, his baton uselessly beating at a distance as he chivvied along other couples to join them. He reached Miss Hawkins' table, and she prayed that he would by-pass them. And indeed he saw them as unlikely candidates and quickly went by, scanning the tables for more likely material. Miss Hawkins would have liked to dance, but she decided she would not suggest it. She hadn't budgeted for dancing and it was up to Brian to make a free offer. But he was silent.

"That was a nice picture," Miss Hawkins said in an attempt to change a subject that had been unspoken.

"I liked the old man best," Brian said.

"Bit of a tyrant, wasn't he?"

"I didn't think so. All he wanted was respect. That's not tyrannical."

"But they won in the end," Miss Hawkins triumphed.

"But the old man didn't lose, did he?" Brian said. "What won in that picture was respect." Brian marvelled at his sudden profundity.

"You set a lot of store by respect, don't you?" Miss Hawkins said.

"The world would be a happier place." Then, after a pause, he took the plunge. "I'm not interested in anybody who doesn't respect me," he said pompously.

"Oh, I do," Miss Hawkins obliged, "I really do. I'd do anything for you, Brian," she said. She heard her nest-egg cracking, but managed a smile. Brian was pleased. She knew what was expected of her. He had laid his cards squarely on the table.

They gave the waiter their order. Two set teas with one Welsh rarebit as an extra. Brian was more than content. His discovery of Miss Hawkins as a willing and paying slave had offered him on a plate the role of master that had been for ever denied him. In his working life, through lack of drive, ambition or perhaps just sheer efficiency, he had remained an underling, and this same menial role had been domestically confirmed. Well, there'd be no more of that, he decided. Even though he wasn't paying the piper, he would certainly call the tune. He caught Miss Hawkins' look of salivating adoration and he was smug with achievement. When the worm turns, that shifting is usually savage, for the bully is but the flip-side of the weakling. Brian needed to perform an act that, cruel as it might seem to others, would confirm for himself his creeping notions of superman.

He looked around the room and his eye rested on a single woman sipping her tea at a corner table. "There's time for a dance," he said. He rose, and Miss Hawkins hesitated. She didn't associate Brian with dancing, and besides, it was not like him to come to such a positive decision. But she shifted in her chair and was on the point of rising.

"Excuse me," Brian said, and he was gone, threading his way to the lone lady across the room. Miss Hawkins remained half-standing, totally bewildered by his behaviour and grinding her jaw in fury as she watched him offer his dancing services to a stranger. She clutched at her chair and sat down. She saw how the two of them almost trotted to the dancing section, and how he circled her waist and clumsily led her around the floor. She crossed her ankles tightly, painfully pressing on a bone, and she heartily wished that her knitting were handy. She could hardly believe what he had done and had a mind there and then to get up and go, and would have done just that had not the music suddenly stopped and she watched him take leave of the lady on the floor.

He returned to the table and sat down as if nothing were amiss. "That's given me an appetite," he said, as the waiter arrived and placed his rarebit before him. Miss Hawkins was too astonished to protest, and as she unlocked her ankles, she felt a movement on her knee. She lifted the tablecloth to find his hand lying there. She could not understand what was happening. Hardly had he settled down after one aberration, he was proceeding with another. But understanding was not the priority. First she had to deal with her feelings, feelings that were so overwhelming that she feared some unnatural change in her body, and feared it with an awful joy. I am enjoying myself, she had to admit, and even if he withdrew his hand at that very moment, she could, in all honesty, tick off that precarious order. And when he was assured of her delight, he put his hand to the cutting of his rarebit. She still felt his hand's fevered imprint on her knee-cap and she was convinced that underneath her stocking lay the spoor of the devil's hoof. Her cheeks were on fire, and she kept her face averted, as if to face him would be an indecent exposure of pleasure. Brian munched at his rarebit, but he noted with satisfaction that he had pleased her.

"You liked that?" he said.

"Do it again, Brian," she said to the tablecloth.

"That was a free sample," he said. As the words came out, he heard their promising implications, and they astonished him. Had he, by some happy chance, come upon some new career for himself, one that he could profit by, and perhaps even enjoy? He eyed her to gauge her reaction, and from her sudden intake of breath, he knew that she'd got the message. Thereafter they ate in silence. Too many questions crowded her mind, and each more perverse than the other. And in her mind were the answers, too unnatural for the telling. So only silence could cover their unspoken and unspeakable dialogue. But Miss Hawkins was thinking and concentrating very hard. If indeed she had to pay for her pleasures, as Brian's statement had clearly inferred, such pleasure would be pure and untrammelled. Miss Hawkins firmly believed that nothing was for nothing, and any pleasure purloined for free was bound to be adulterated with guilt and shame. No sin could be attached to pleasure if it had been earned with good and hard cash. Indeed, through such a transaction, pleasure would amount to a virtue. It now seemed to Miss Hawkins to be totally immoral to accept a complimentary pass to happiness. It was incumbent on her, as a good Christian, to foot the bill of her gratification.

When they had finished, the waiter handed Brian the bill, and he, without embarrassment, passed it across the table.

"I enjoyed that very much," he said, assuring her that her investment was not wasteful. She put a bold face on the bill, taking care not to betray her horror at the offensive total. The change from the broken five-pound note would just about cover it, and quickly she recalled the hell-born print on her knee-cap to offset her dismay. She put the exact money on the plate, covering it with the bill. She had no money for a tip, and she was anxious to leave the room before the waiter returned. She got up from the table, and Brian followed. In the street, he took her arm.

"I'd like to see you again," he said.

"What about your mother?"

"I'll fix her," he said with a bully's courage. "Next Friday then?"

She did not answer immediately. She was trying to recall what was due on her pension.

"I'll have something for you," he said.

"What's that?"

Brian hesitated. A price-list was what he had in mind to surprise her with, but he could not state it so crudely. "It'll be a sort of menu," he said, suddenly inspired by the recollection of the yellow-rose bill of fare in the café. "And I'll decorate it, too," he laughed. "With roses, perhaps. I'm not a bad painter."

"What sort of things will it have?"

They had reached the bus-stop, and he did not answer straightaway, taking his stand at the end of the queue. "What sort of things?" she said again.

He bent down to her ear. "Things I know you like," he whispered.

His hot breath seared her with its fire, and she shook with the thrill of such intimacy.

"All kinds of items," he said. "Little and big."

"And what they cost?" she said. She wanted to make it clear that she wanted nothing for nothing.

"It's only a game, really," Brian said. "I'll put it all by for you. It'll be a way of saving."

"For what?" she said, in as casual a tone as her rising hopes would allow.

"Well, you never can tell," he said. "Of course," he added, sure enough of his ground, "it may not be the kind of game you want to play."

"Have you played it before?" she said. She hoped it didn't sound as if she suspected his motives in any way.

"Of course not," he said truly enough. "We're both beginners, and we'll have to learn from each other."

"How will you know about the prices?" she said innocently.

"Well, we'll start with the smallest item, and say that'll be two-pence and then we'll grade it upwards. Oh, it's exciting," he said.

She saw his bus in the distance. He bent down and pecked her on her ear. Miss Hawkins practically collapsed from her body fever. "Another free sample," he laughed. "To-day is opening day."

She was glad when the bus arrived. She leaned against the stop-post, watching him board and waving good-bye. She stayed there long after the bus had disappeared, then, exhausted, she made her way home. Once arrived, she flopped into the armchair without the strength to take off her coat. And sitting there, she relived each seething moment of his various assaults. Her detailed recall did little to lessen her fatigue, which was so acute that it even overcame her strong urge to reach for her diary and tick off the day's orders. So she rested for a while, trying to close her mind to all the events of the afternoon. She concentrated on her penniless state, and this helped to dull the edge of her fatigue. Then, opening her diary, she read the orders aloud. She had fulfilled each one to the letter, and in token of her sense of achievement, she underlined her obedience with a double red tick. She thought of Brian, and saw him, paint-brush in hand, scrolling his price-list with yellow petals. She smiled. She, too, would have to attend to her hus-bandry.

She took a piece of paper and divided it with a bold line into two columns which she headed Income and Expenditure. Her pension was adequate for living expenses and to pay off the diminishing mortgage on her flat. The interest accumulating on her nest-egg she put aside for pleasures, but she had no notion of whether or not it would be adequate. Her demands were avid, but as yet she had no guidance as to the supply, though she suspected that it would outstrip the available interest. Then she set to wondering what was the purpose of keeping the nest-egg intact. In her will it was written that it was ear-marked for the Orphanage, simply because there seemed no other purpose for it. Now she saw such a bequest as a folly in the extreme, and that she owed nothing to that grey prison of her purl and plain recollection. And that to spite it she must squander every penny. Indeed so impatient was she to embark on her profligate life that she began to list what she was prepared to pay for Brian's services. She had no difficulty in imagining what they would be, detail by detail, but her thoughts shamed her as her excited agitation grew. So perverse were they that they were not for speaking aloud and certainly not for registering in indelible pencil. She grabbed her knitting and stitched herself into some modicum of calm. There were five whole days to wait till Friday. Most of the time would be consumed with her knitting, and she would give her diary a few days' rest. This decision pleased her. Though her diary had become an indispensable companion to her daily life, it irritated her sometimes, as she feared its power and her dependency. This week she would call the tune, and the diary would have to hold its dangerous tongue. It would be liberating to live alone for a while again. Maurice, too, would stay on the floor, and she would spend her days in isolated anticipation of an unknown and perhaps perilous future.

7

MRS. WATTS HAD NOTICED A DISTINCT CHANGE IN HER SON AND she was not sure that it pleased her. For the last few days not a word of protest or petulance had escaped him. He did his duty by her without complaint, with grace even, and though she should have found such treatment an agreeable change, there was something about his manner that unnerved her. She was not anxious as to why he had changed: that was his business, and whatever was happening to him was of no interest to her. Except in so far as it affected herself and her own well-being. She had never liked her son. His untimely, unwished for arrival had been the cause of her marriage in the first place, and she never quite forgave him for forcing her into a contract to which both parties were equally unwilling. But when Brian was born, she thought the three of them could make some kind of life together. She had never looked forward to the novelty of wife and motherhood, and she had been both for two short months before Mr. Watts, who already had little appetite for his position, sensed a displacement even in that, and one evening while she was feeding, he packed a bag and simply disappeared. He left a note on the bedside table in case she should wait up for him. When Mrs. Watts had finished the feeding, she called to her not much better half, and hearing no reply, she entertained three possibilities. One, he was not answering because for some reason he was angry with her; two, that he had slipped out for a quick pint at the pub; or three, that he had simply dropped dead. She milled over all the possibilities and had to admit to herself that in truth she wished for the last. She went to the foot of the stairs. She noticed that his coat was gone from the stand, and with regret she acknowledged that he must have gone to the pub. She carried the baby to the cot which was kept alongside her side of the bed. She caught sight of the note on the bedside table and instinctively knew that her marriage was at an end. Fearfully she read it. "I've gone for good," he had written. "Can't stand it any longer." Mrs. Watts was too vain a woman to consider that the "it" that he couldn't stand had anything to do with her. The "it," without doubt, was Brian. She practically threw him into the cot. By some miraculous survival instinct, he made no protest, which was just as well, for she might there and then have smothered him. For her anger was loud and extreme. A few minutes ago she had wished for a respectable widowhood and a cashing-in of the life-insurance she had nagged him into taking out on their wedding-day. Now her status was that of a humiliated desertee, and she looked at the silent, frightened bundle in the cot with loathing. The look was not lost on little Brian, and he took this opportunity to donate to the world his first smile, and with it, he was pleading for his life. Her heart softened towards him long enough to stay her hand, and this negative offering was the first and last tenderness she ever gave him. Thereafter she suffered him. Suffered his wetting, his teething, his crying, his fevers, and throughout his child and boyhood, she envisaged all means of getting shot of him. Until he threatened independence. At that moment, she decided to keep him by her. He had ruined her life. Now, whether he liked it or not, he would pay for it with companionship, and later on, with care. There had been times when it seemed he might leave her. The army had been the most threatening competitor, but her sudden and well-timed bouts of genuine ill-health had secured him by her side. After the war, she had pushed him into a job of shop-assistant in an art shop, simply because it was near the house and enabled him to get back to make her lunch. He hadn't minded it too much, for painting had been his hobby for many years. He stayed there till his retirement. He'd never been promoted, and during his time, many younger than he by-passed him to management. But as far as his mother was concerned, he earned enough to keep them both, and his bitterness was entirely of his own making. On two occasions, the comforts of Mrs. Watts's old age had been threatened by daughters-in-law, and for each of them she invented stories about her son's inadequacies. The last suitor, an overbearing lady called Eileen, was not put off by reports of Brian's selfishness and brutality, but finally gave up the fight on Mrs. Watts's suggestion of her son's homosexuality. Though she didn't use the word. She had read in books that some men made love to other men. She didn't believe one filthy word of it, but it was certainly worth a try. The hardy Eileen, who was prepared to put up with any shortcomings for the sake of matrimony, finally drew the line at that obstruction and no more was seen of her.

From that time onwards, Brian had made small movements of protest, which over the years became more frequent and disagreeable. He hardly ever smiled and never at her. That survival weapon was long obsolete. Over the latter years, he had gone about her geriatric business with disgust and silent loathing. But Mrs. Watts took no offence at it. That's how men were, so his behaviour was in no way surprising. But things had changed. Over the last few days, she had caught him smiling to himself, and she felt threatened, for she preferred the sullen battle to the complaisant peace. His smile indicated some scheme afoot, or worse, a recollection of a secret life of which she had no part. She watched him from the corner of the room where she was pretending to read her library book. He was writing on a large sheet of drawing-paper, and he was licking his lips and smiling the while. Suddenly she could not stand her isolation, and she shouted at him that she wanted a cup of tea, though she had no appetite for it, but she could not countenance a moment of his non-attention. He got up straightaway, taking care to cover the parchment sheet with a piece of blotter. Now she knew for certain that he had a secret and she was determined to

find out what preoccupation so excluded her. She heard him running the water in the kitchen and she gauged that she had enough
time to cross over to his desk, satisfy her curiosity and return to her
library book. But she was a slow mover, and a careful one, for she
did not want to run the risk of breaking her brittle bones and give
him an excuse for putting her away. Sometimes, in dark moments,
he had threatened it: "It'll be the Twilight Home for you," he
would say. And it was a nightmarish threat. She had heard about
the home from the woman upstairs who'd put her mother there, and
now the old widow from downstairs was going there, too, and she
would be left, redundant on the middle floor, a disgrace to the
young house with her age and incontinence. She didn't want to go
to the Twilight Home, and the fear of it locked her step towards his
desk. She sat down again. No. She didn't want to be cooped up in a
ward with a dozen smelling women who didn't know how to control themselves. And to have the occasional visitor who couldn't
wait to get away. Sometimes she day-dreamed about The Petunias,
the posh home for senior citizens that she'd read about in one of the
Sunday papers. It was like she imagined a hotel would be, with
thick carpets on every inch of floor and your own private bathroom
a few steps away from your bed. And meals brought by servants at
a touch of a bell, and a colour television all to yourself. She would
like that, she thought. For that kind of luxury she would gladly get
out of her son's way. But The Petunias was for the rich, and would
remain for her forever a day-dream.

"Hurry up with the tea," she shouted in her frustration, and she
spat on the threadbare carpet in disgust.

Brian returned with the tea-tray. He set it down on the table, then
went straight to the concealing piece of blotting paper to check that
it hadn't been moved. Mrs. Watts sensed a deep belligerence in
him, and she was glad she had decided against prying into his affairs. She saw him smile again, and did not know how much longer
she could stand it. She gave a sigh for The Petunias, and screamed
at him: "What are you smiling about?" she said.

"D'you have to know everything?"

His words were a hopeful sign of a renewed battle, but he was smiling even as he said them. It was clear he was giving nothing away.

"You're plotting against me," she said. "You're writing a letter to the Twilight Home. You're asking about vacancies."

He picked up the drawing-sheet. It was unreadable from her distance, but it was clear enough that the writing was in the form of a list. "Does that look like a letter?" he said, still smiling.

She regretted that she hadn't smothered him in his cot all those years ago. "It's the list of things I have to take with me," she said, needing desperately to kindle the flicker of a fight. "I won't need much in the Twilight Home," she said. "They even provide a night-dress. White state flannel," she said, "and state slippers and yellow state soap. I've heard all about it," she said. "Well, I'm not going," she screamed at him. "I'll call the police."

He removed his smile and it seemed to calm her a little. "Who said anything about the Twilight Home?" he said.

"There isn't another one," she sulked. Then, after a pause, "Except The Petunias." She looked at him and saw a sly smile flit across his face, and it was clearly a smile for her and not on account of some private recollection. "You'd have to rob a bank," she said, and she heard herself laughing.

He poured her the tea. "I was thinking of taking a part-time job," he said. "They need someone in the children's library after school. Three days a week."

"We can manage on what we've got," she said, on her guard.

"Thought I'd like to get out a bit," he said. "You could be left on your own for a few hours."

In view of her softened feelings towards him, she agreed, though she knew that there would be times when she would resent his non-attendance. "What will I get out of it?" she said.

"My happiness." It astounded him that he articulated such a thought to his mother who, in her turn, had no notion of how to deal with it. Her son's happiness had never been any of her business, and that it should give her pleasure was a notion that she had never entertained. She thought about it for a while, and couldn't, for all her trying, make any connexion. "The least you can do is bring me home some chocolates," she said.

"Is it alright then?"

"You're sure it's a job?"

"I'll show you my wages if you like, and I'll save them up," he said.

"What for?"

He smiled again, and this time it was for himself. "Well, you never know," he said. He was glad that he had manoeuvred his working hours so easily, and he was anxious to get back to his list which would form the working basis of his income. He sat at his desk and perused the services he had so far itemized. As yet, he'd not priced them, but he'd listed them in degrees of titillation according to his inexperienced but hotly imagined standards. So that the holding of Miss Jean Hawkins' hand was the first offer on the list, and in such a position would be the cheapest service. He reckoned he could hardly charge more than 2p. for that one, and certainly not less, for that would undervalue his craft. Next came the holding of two hands, which logically should have cost double, but he was afraid to escalate too soon, for he could imagine so many items on the ladder of her affections that the cost of the final service on the top rung would surely be prohibitive. So he put the double handhold at 3p. and hoped she'd have the sense to smell a bargain. These two leading items he had wreathed in yellow rose-petals and underlined with a green leaf. The leaf signalled the beginning of a more specialized line of service, and a consequently higher price. Heading these special services were those parts of the body not necessarily visible to the naked eye, and included a fondling of the elbow, neck and ankle, and the knee. These items he decorated with rosebuds, with their inbuilt promise of total bloom, which would be found in the next section. This third category was the most daring, and he intended to frame it in an outline of brown thorns. He had not yet itemized this section, for he knew it would take time and called on all his ingenuity to describe each service in graphic yet subtle terms, and to come to a decision regarding the fees. Meanwhile he contented himself with painting the frame of thorns. The thorn motif he'd chosen for its implication of pain, but the pain was to be sweetened by the occasional yellow rose in full and bursting bloom. And there would be dew on each petal. He didn't know why, but he sensed that this small detail would be appropriate. He set to work on the illustration while Mrs. Watts, shackled with prejudice, considered the implications of his part-time job. All that she could think of were the drawbacks, the hours of loneliness and non-attention. But the one bonus that she could reap from the situation was the knowledge that he would be out of the house long enough for her to rummage through his papers and discover what schemes he was making on her behalf. For despite his denials, the threat of the Twilight Home loomed its dark shadow.

"When do you start your job?" she said, anxious to make a start on her reconnaissance.

"Next Friday." His answer was prompt. "For an hour or so." He intended to meet Miss Hawkins as arranged and to present her with the bill of fare. He would hand it to her and suggest she take it home for her consideration. He would be too embarrassed to be witness to her perusal and her first reactions which he could not quite predict. He would arrange to meet her on Monday afternoon. Perhaps with luck she might invite him to her house, for most of his supplies, apart from those in the first category, were certainly not alfresco. By Friday morning he would have completed his full trade-list. He found it difficult to concentrate on the imagined specialities while his mother was in the room. Her eavesdropping presence made of his ledger an obscenity. He made a mental note to take it with him wherever he went, and not to risk making a copy. He would give the original to Miss Hawkins, and suggest that she should keep it for him, framed, if she so wished, above her mantelpiece, so that she was constantly aware of the price of her pleasure.

He felt his mother staring at him, and sensed how his secret smile displeased her. So he was not surprised when she shouted across the room, with all her spiteful triumph: "I've wet," she said. Wearily he crossed over to her chair and helped her into the bathroom. Then he took a cloth from the kitchen and mopped the floor. Sometimes he thought that she did it on purpose, and as he wiped away, keeping his face averted, his mind was filled with thoughts that always seemed to accompany every mopping-up operation as to how much longer it would be before he could decently put her away. And by decently, he meant a time when, in utter ignorance, she would not know where or how she resided. He would have to wait for total senility. He wished her body health for as long as she lived, but he wished her, too, an infant's innocence and trust that was unavailable to the pain of humiliation. He was waiting for the time when she would not know him, when one morning he would take her cup of tea and she would ask him his name. Often he day-dreamed such an occurrence. He would then, without scruple, dress her with infinite care and tenderness and take her in a car to the Twilight Home and she would never know who had discarded her. And he would visit her weekly and feel no offence at her non-recognition. He couldn't bring himself to do it while she was full of blood and verbal memory, and every day he listened for non sequiturs and inconsequential prattle. Yet he had heard that senility could not be relied on, that some old people, even in their nineties, had gone raging into dying as if the poor offended world still owed them a living. He listened to her stockinged tread from the bedroom, he riled with every inch of her terrible caution, and he began to question her entitlement to survive at all. But such thoughts were painful to him, and quickly he took the mop into the kitchen and rinsed it under the cold water. Till next time, he told himself, and the next, and he wondered on the quality of incontinence among the posh people at The Petunias and whether it contained an inbuilt upper class discretion. He heard her coming from her bedroom, and he went to help her back into her chair.

"Don't do it again," he said. He always said that after each mopping-up, though he knew there was no point in it, because in a disgusting way, she couldn't help herself.

"You won't send me away, will you?" she said, but there was little fear in her voice and less sincerity, but she said it after each accident just to let him know that she knew very well what was in his mind.

"Of course not," he said, as he always answered her, but his answer clearly referred to this time, and this time only, and held no assurance that his tolerance was infinite.

"I wonder how much it costs at The Petunias?" she said.

"Thought you didn't want to be put away?"

"The Petunias isn't putting away. It's like living in a hotel for ever."

"How d'you know? You've never been to a hotel."

"I've seen them on television."

"Wouldn't you miss me?" he said.

"You could visit me sometimes. I'd let you have a hot bath in my private bathroom."

"Well you can forget it," he said. "It costs too much."

"You're getting a job," she said.

He didn't answer at once. He needed a moment to consider the idea she had just planted in his mind. And to remember for always that it was she who had first thought of it. The small moneys he expected to receive from Miss Hawkins in payment of his services had, until that moment, no special purpose in his mind. The odd new shirt for himself, or a box of chocolates for his mother, was all he expected his immoral earnings to cover. But his mother, innocent of his part-time vocation, had unawares thrust him into trade. If there were one Miss Hawkins, there were plenty more, and libraries galore in which to trap them. He would go public, he decided. He would design half a dozen bills of fare, each one with a different motif, and he would fling his net wide to avoid discovery. He reckoned that with half a dozen regular and well-paying clients, his mother could be kept at The Petunias till the end of her days. And he would always remember that it was she who first put the idea in his mind. He marvelled that such a frayed and failing body still harboured such cunning and clarity of mind.

"Well you never know," he said. He made a note to investigate the prices at The Petunias. Perhaps there was a cheap rate if you had a room without your own bathroom. He hardly saw the point in it anyway, since, as far as her body's natural functions were concerned, his mother was sublimely indifferent to location. The thought of his new career excited him. It would be hard and exhausting work, but he would be calling on resources that he had never exploited and would surely demand and receive that respect which all his life had been denied him. And he would be doing it for his mother. The fact that it would be an act of such sacrifice robbed it of its overtones of sin. There was nothing more that a good son could do. He thought of Miss Hawkins with tenderness. None of his clients must ever be aware of the existence of the others. He would divide his time between them as equally as their appetites and purses would allow. But Miss Hawkins would occupy a special place in his heart as being his first and loyal customer. He could barely wait till Friday to open his shop.

Meanwhile, he had much work to do. His business could not expand by personal recommendation. Each customer had to be picked and vetted. A couple of miles from his house was a special gramaphone record library housed in the Town Hall. Women who lived alone were as dependent on records as on books or cats. It could be a happy hunting-ground.

"Think I'll go for a walk," he said to his mother.

"Where to?"

"The park or something. Get some fresh air."

She hoped he'd leave his list behind on the desk, but as she was wishing it, he picked it up and rolled it under his arm.

"Won't be long," he said, and he was out before she could protest. She fumed after him, stamping her foot like a petulant child. "Going to plot against me," she shouted after him. In his absence she intended to work herself into a ripe fury so that she could make a good and proper mess by the time he got home.

8

WHEN FRIDAY CAME, MISS HAWKINS HAD KNITTED A GOOD THREE feet of scarf. Her green rage had diluted to a pale blue, then to yellow and finally petered out into a calm off-white. She was at peace with herself. Her ignorance as to what the future held for her had finally blunted the edge of her excitement, and put a stop to her fanciful guesswork that was based on so little information. By Friday her mind was open and available to all experience. She put Maurice back on the wall with the intention of dining with him that evening so that she could tell him, detail by detail, of Brian's programme and use him as a sounding-board for advice. Then she was faced with the diary. She opened it and flicked through the week's pages. Since her last meeting with Brian, she had simply recorded what she had done, and each page was filled in at the end of its day. Thus she had risen, breakfasted, lunched and dined, read, knitted, cleaned the flat and looked at television. It was a week's entry that any diligent, dull schoolgirl would have been proud of. Reading it, she thought how dull it was, and she turned back to the very beginning of her sentence and read the entries with shame. She marvelled at the change that had come over her in the months that had passed since her retirement. She hardly recognized the fearful soul who had risen and eaten so precisely. And had done absolutely nothing else. She was aware of a terrible wastage. Indeed not only of the days since her retirement but of her entire life that had consisted in fulfilling duties prescribed by others without one hint of her own initiative. If, as a child, she had had half the daring that she had presently acquired, she would have broken out of the Orphanage prison. Such thoughts made her reach again for her knitting, but so strong was her present control that it took only one line of off-white plaining to dispel them. She put her knitting down and wondered how she would fill her diary for the day. Though she had enjoyed her week's freedom from the diary's orders, she knew that such freedom entailed the dreariness of predictability. For the whole of her life, that had been the norm, and there had never been a break in the pattern. Nowadays that norm was as a holiday. Today she would return to the exacting job of living. But what orders should she dictate? Because she had no idea of what to expect, she couldn't stretch its possibilities by any diary challenge. All she knew was that she would be called upon to spend money. If she ordered herself to overspend, that would incur no risk except that of penury. But to bargain with his prices without being able to use the threat of going elsewhere, that was a challenging order and its ticking off would give infinite pleasure. So she wrote, "Halved Brian's prices." She read it over, and then considered that she might be thought cheese-paring. So she added the rider, "without being unfair." She intended to go to the bank before meeting Brian and to take out a sum rather larger than her weekly allowance. She expected that he would want payment in cash, for such earnings were hardly declarable income. Perhaps on her way to the library she would be bold enough to enter the private bar of the local pub where she had once been on a workers' party outing. It was a sedate place where women on their own could take a quiet drink without being molested. She had never been in a pub on her own before, so it was a challenge worth ordering in her diary. So on the line above her bargaining orders, for she valued a respect for chronology, she wrote, "Went to the Pirate's Arms. Had a gin and lime." She had no idea how gin and lime tasted, but from her reading she knew that it was the correct drink for a woman of her station. She shut the diary partly because the gesture represented a completed job of work, and partly for the pleasure of opening it on her return and of reading once again her day's orders before confirming them with her red crayon. She opened the wardrobe for her coat and found its empty swinging hanger. She realized that it still lay on the settee. She thought to herself that she was getting slovenly. Yet for some reason, it didn't displease her. On the contrary, it gave her a strong sense of liberation that such trivia no longer obsessed her. As she put it on, she noticed that the sleeve lining was untacked, and it almost pleased her, and as a final rebellion she went out into the street where everybody could see, without bothering to do up the bone buttons. Miss Hawkins was well on the way to going bohemian.

When she reached the Pirate's Arms, she hovered for a while outside, and as some kind of self-protection, she buttoned her coat. She went inside. On each side of the vestibule there was a door. A lot of noise seemed to be coming from the door on her right, so she tried the left one and found herself in a small parlour. About a half a dozen people sat quietly at tables, most of them women on their own, and she felt reassured. She took a seat. There were no waiters in evidence, and she wondered whether it was up to her to fetch her order from the bar. She was too shy to cross the room under the gaze of the other loners, yet to stay sitting where she was, with seemingly no purpose, might draw equal attention on herself. She hesitated, and the barman, who had been watching her, caught her eye. He trapped her gaze for a moment, and then, with the high disdain of his calling, he enquired across the bar, and in full earshot of all his customers, "Port and lemon, madam?" She was too frightened to deny it. She had no idea what it was but it sounded contemptible, a fit combination to offset the obvious inadequacies of her sort of person. She felt assaulted, but as if in answer to an order, she nodded her head. He turned his back and poured it, then placed it on the bar. She rose, and in her nervousness pushed back the chair on which she was sitting and it fell over with a loud clang on the linoed floor. "I'm sorry," she said to everybody and to nobody in particular. She bent to pick up the chair, and as she straightened up, she felt dizzy, and the distance between herself and the bar seemed to have widened considerably. The small, isolated port and lemon had become an alcoholic's blur. She held on to the table to steady herself, and heartily wished she'd never set foot in the place. She staggered over to the bar and collected her potion.

"Forty pence," the barman said before she could take it away.

She had to make a return trip for her handbag, which she'd left on the table, and as she picked it up, a surge of anger fuelled her, and she wished she had brought her knitting. She paid for her drink and brought it back to the table. She sipped it gingerly—at 4op. a go, she intended to savour it slowly—and as she relished it, for it was a new and exciting taste, she recalled the order in her diary. It had been specific. A gin and lime had been its undeniable prescription, and it was an act of disobedience to modulate it in any way. Yet the port and lemon had been by way of an order, too. The barman had made that clear, and confused, she wondered how many masters she was serving. Yet the diary's orders, she knew, superseded all, and she downed her drink and went boldly to the bar.

"A gin and lime," she said with sudden new-found authority.

The barman raised an eyebrow. He smiled, but not disdainfully. There was a small flicker of respect in his smile, the respect for a hard and dedicated drinker. Miss Hawkins liked his smile no better than his former contempt, for both were indications of total misunderstanding. "How much?" she said, before he could inform her. It was she who was master now, and she enjoyed the sudden role-reversal.

"Forty pence," he said.

"And a slice of lemon," she added, homing in on her new-found authority, though she had no idea whether lemon was a fit extra ingredient.

The barman nodded, both in obedience and agreement. "I'll bring it to your table," he said.

For the first time in her life Miss Hawkins felt served. This new experience quite confounded her and led her to speculate on the series of masters she had served all her life. The first was the one who encapsulated them all and there was no need to scour further afield than the Sacred Heart Orphanage to catch the whiff of authority. Again she longed for her knitting, and as an alternative, she took a generous swig of her gin and lime. The mixture throbbed lustily in her throat, and startled her. How had she managed all her life to miss out on this bacchanalian adventure? And as she swallowed it, she relished the exciting threat of addiction. She had to admit that her recent moment of authority at the bar had been glorious. The satisfaction it engendered was as great as that which accompanied the ticking off of an order. She set to thinking that to command was as splendid as to serve and she realized that in her anticipated role with Brian, she would be master and call each tune. It's true she would be paying for his services, but that would in no way disturb the balance of the status of master and slave. She would pay him as a grand lady would give wages to her personal maid, for humanity's sake. She was getting the best of two worlds, she decided. She would have Brian at her purse's beck and call, but her own service she would devote exclusively to her diary, and that small green book, which occasionally she loathed for its tyranny, now appeared to her as an object of worship. She was in all ways, she felt, well and truly blessed, and as a toast to her good fortune, she downed her gin and lime. She was feeling quite heady, and spirited enough to consider another order. But she decided against it, not out of meanness or self-discipline, but because she feared that Brian might smell the beginnings of her fall. For fall it was, of that she was sure, and she cared little about it, for a self-indulging drinking habit seemed to be a natural accompaniment to the enslavement she had in mind. For the rest of her life she would go gloriously to pieces in a pursuit of innocent debauchery and diary idolatry.

She got up from the table and made her way to the door. She walked slowly, sensing that her legs were faintly unreliable. Outside in the open air, she had to lean against the door, taking in gulps of fresh air to offset her sudden nausea. She recalled how once in the Orphanage she had eaten two helpings of pudding, the second, surreptitiously, for it had been Dodds's share. Dodds had a tapioca allergy which Matron could never tolerate. Hawkins had done Dodds a favour, so that when Matron came round after dinner, Dodds had proudly shown her empty plate. But Hawkins had heaved with sickness, and her sudden pallor did not escape Matron's beady eye. She recalled Dodds's tapioca aversion and looked at her platter wiped clean. Beside it was Hawkins' green face, and Matron lost no time in putting the two facts together. "Come with me, both of you," she said, and tremblingly they followed her to the cloak-room where Matron placed Hawkins in the middle of the stone floor. "Open your mouth wide," she said, "and stick your finger down your throat."

"I can't," Hawkins dared to suggest, preferring the disease to such a monstrous cure.

"Do as I say," Matron said.

"Go on, Hawkins," Dodds said timidly from the side-lines. Had she had an idea of what was to be her punishment, she would have pleaded with Hawkins to keep a strong hold on every lump of the offending tapioca inside her, but she feared that Matron's possible wrath with Hawkins could only increase her anger towards herself. "Go on, Hawkins," she pleaded.

Now, standing alone in the middle of that cold stone floor, it seemed that everyone was against her, and there was no point in living any more, so she might as well choke herself, because that was what she truly felt Matron was ordering her to do. She sent a swift and silent prayer to her Maker, and did as Matron asked. Almost immediately she retched, and threw up her spurt of misplaced generosity onto the floor. Immediately she felt better, and so grateful was she for the relief that she was on the point of thanking Matron, when, looking up, she saw her gazing at Dodds and connecting her with the mess on the floor.

"Now get a cloth, Dodds, and clean it up," Matron said.

Miss Hawkins wondered how poor Dodds had come to terms with that orphan-experience, and whether she, too, was knitting a scarf without end.

She managed to walk to the corner of the street and into a narrow alley. There she applied Matron's cure, knowing the relief it would bring, and in no danger of feeling grateful to its source. She was careful not to soil her clothes, so she kept her person as far as possible from her relief, and when it was over, she wiped her mouth, unbuttoned her coat and walked out of the alley, leaving Dodds's work to the rain, cats, or simply time. In her bag she always carried packets of peppermints and indigestion tablets. She took one each of these, and relished the purging relief they gave. She walked to the bank, breathing deeply and with her mouth open to rid herself of any tell-tale odour. In the bank she tried to write out a cash cheque without looking, as if someone else were overdrawing on her account. But for legibility's sake she was obliged to keep one eye open, so that the £25 she was donating to herself appeared as a blur, and fogged the sin of extravagance. Normally she would take the five separate pounds of her weekly allowance and press them neatly into her wallet. She always insisted on clean, unwrinkled notes which reflected her profound respect for hard-earned cash. Now she took the notes and stuffed them without ceremony into her handbag. She had no intention of itemizing her expenditures as was her custom. All she knew was that its disposal would be more ritualistic than its collection, and the less she thought about it, the better.

Brian was waiting for her outside the library. She noticed that he was smiling, and somehow she felt that the smile was not prepared for herself. His smile was internal, and he was possibly unaware of the creases on his face or his look of benign cordiality. When he saw her, he stiffened, as with sudden stage-fright, and the smile was forced now, and produced.

"Hullo, Brian," she said. She was careful to keep her distance in case the gin-port-lemon-lime concoction still hovered on her breath, then she went to his side and took his arm. "Where shall we go?" she said.

"I can't stay long to-day," Brian said quickly, "my mother's not too well."

She should have said she was sorry, but all the regret she felt was that his mother was not ill enough. "Oh, I was so looking forward," she said.

"But I've got something for you," he said. He took a large folder from out of the inside of his coat. She made to take it from him, but he held it back. "No," he said, "it's for you to look at when I'm gone."

"Is it the—" She wondered whether there was a legitimate name for what the folder contained.

"Yes," he said, "it's what I promised."

She remembered the order in her diary. It was imperative that she see the list, otherwise there could be no bargaining. "Oh, let me see it now," she said.

He shook his head emphatically.

"Please," she said, but she could see that he was adamant. "Alright," she said, risking it, "then I won't take it at all."

He didn't answer, but it was clear her response disturbed him. "Let's sit down in the park," he said.

So they walked in silence. Miss Hawkins was confident she would finally get her way, while Brian searched in his mind for some valid reason why she should not see the bill of fare. In desperation, he thought he might try the truth.

They sat down on a bench. "I'm ready now," she said, settling herself.

"I can't show it to you. Not in front of me," he said.

"Turn your back, then."

"It's not that. I just don't want to be present."

"Why ever not?"

He looked away and to the trees that bordered the park. He said, "It's sort of embarrassing."

She took his hand. "It's embarrassing for me, too," she said, "but like you said last time, we're both beginners."

"You can see the first two parts of it," he said, still not looking at her.

She reasoned that her diary would be satisfied. "Alright," she said, "that's a fair compromise."

He took the folder out of his coat, and hiding it from her view, he folded over the first offerings of his price-list, and laid it squarely on her lap. Then he got up. "I'll go for a bit of a walk," he said.

"Suit yourself," she said, though she was glad to be left alone. She waited until he had gone some distance and out of earshot of her tremblings, and she fixed her eyes on the parchment sheet. The yellow roses impressed her enough to make her dwell long on their iridescent tear-drops of dew. She thought Brian was very romantic, and she looked up from the sheet of paper and watched him weaving his way through the trees like a poet, she thought, in search of inspiration. Hers was a pure and innocent appraisal, which was just as well, since it would act as a bulwark to the shock of the yellow roses' copy. She laid her hand over the whole section, lowering it item by item.

The first service read as follows: "To holding of hand, 2p." And bracketed underneath was written, "To holding of two hands, 3p." She appreciated the reduction and thought that altogether it was a fair enough price for a gesture that gave her so much pleasure. Despite the diary, she felt it unfair to bargain on that item. Then she set to thinking whether he meant 2p. each time, or whether that payment sufficed for each meeting. If she once let go of his hand, did she have to pay again to reclaim it? If such were the case, her whole nest-egg would evaporate on handholding. She resolved to clarify that item as soon as Brian returned. She looked up and saw him in the distance. His back was towards her. Then he stopped and slowly turned his head. He caught her watching him, and quickly he turned away and walked briskly to the far end of the park. He was clearly delaying his return. She was glad, for she needed the time. She would insist that the hand-holding would be a single payment that covered the whole of each meeting. Then her diary would be satisfied. She lowered her hand to discover the next item. Her eye went first to the price column which had escalated considerably. For a touching of the elbow (through sleeve) was a princely 20p., a neck-hold was priced at 25, an ankle embrace at 30, and a knee-caress rocketed to 50p. She wondered why the knee was more expensive than the ankle. She personally would have interchanged the prices, but no doubt Brian's lust-gradations reflected more the quality of his appetites than her own. The knee-caress was the last permitted item. The taboos lay beneath the fold. Even though Brian was still some distance away, she was not tempted to take a peep. Besides, she was aware of a fever that crept through her during her perusal of the first items, and she thought it better to keep the rest of the offerings for the privacy of her own sitting-room, with Maurice's face firmly to the wall. She looked up and gauged her voice to the distance between them. "Brian," she shouted, "I'm ready."

He was glad there were few people in the park. Her shouting embarrassed him and it passed through his mind to put up his prices. He was loath to return to the bench and face her hot anticipation of his services. Her blushes would make them obscene and render illicit what was in his view an entirely legitimate bill of sale. Well, she could take it or leave it. The world was full of clients.

He strode aggressively towards her and sat himself by her side. "Well?" he said.

She was astonished at his boldness and lack of reserve. "I like it," she said, "but what about the twopence for holding the hand? Is that for all day?"

"It's for as long as you can hang on," he said.

"Well, I don't think that's very fair," Miss Hawkins said timidly. "I think it should be twopence for each meeting."

Brian was not pleased. If she was capable of bargaining on the smallest item, it was obviously a principle with her, and she would apply it to each available service. He did not feel he could yield. "I think it's a fair enough price," he said.

"But I'd spend all my money on just that one item. I'd have very little left for anything else. And I can guess what that is." She looked away from him and nudged him in the ribs. Brian began to wonder whether she was a client worth wooing. A lifetime of hand-holding with Miss Hawkins could hardly underwrite one week's lodging at The Petunias. He couldn't afford to lose a customer, but it was a blow to his pride to sell his services so cheaply.

"I tell you what," he said, knowing that holding two hands

would be a rare necessity, "you can have the two for the price of one."

She was satisfied. She had obliged her diary's order. He took the parchment and replaced the folder which he put into her hand.

"I've got to go now," he said. "You can take that home and study it. I'll see you on Monday afternoon," he said. He wanted to give her enough time to savour his offerings but not enough to oversavour them, and therefore find his personal participation dispensable. He was aware of being in a tricky line of business.

"Where shall we meet?" she said. Normally it was a redundant question. The library was their accepted rendezvous. But she sensed that their next meeting might require some form of habitation.

He smiled. "Shall I come to your house?" he said.

She gave him the address.

"I'll be there about three o'clock," he said.

"I'll put the kettle on," she said, sensing in advance some need to invent a postponement to the serious business of their meeting.

They parted at the bus-stop. She clutched the folder in her hand. As she passed the pub, the thought of a gin and lime quickly entered her mind and as quickly departed. Not because of the sickness it might entail—that was due to mixing, she was sure—but because she feared by instinct a growing drink dependence. If Brian hadn't entered her life, she might possibly have drunk her five years away into an alcoholic blur. Now she had been offered another addiction, and though possibly more costly, it would not blunt her responses to her enjoyment.

When she reached home, she kneeled on the floor of the sitting-room facing Maurice as he leaned against the wall. "Look what I've got for you," she said, displaying the folder. "It's a secret," she said, "but only for me. One day perhaps, I'll share it with you." She turned him to face the wall, then she opened the diary and read the day's orders aloud. For a while she held the red crayon in her hand, wishing to prolong the gratification, then meticulously she ticked off each order, adding an extra tick to the pub where she felt she had acquitted herself beyond the call of duty. She took off her coat and placed the folder on the dining-room table. She did not want to give herself the comfort of an armchair. She sensed she would need all her wits about her to fathom the subtleties of Brian's list. On the hard dining-chair, she would feel sufficient discomfort to offset the pleasures of her list perusal, which she expected to be overwhelming. And as a practical prelude to the delights that were to come, she read and re-read the first section so that she knew it by heart.

When she was ready for Brian's main course dishes, she drew the curtains in the living-room and switched on a small table-lamp. Then she remembered a bar of milk chocolate in the cupboard, one left over from a number she had bought on the day of her first meeting with Brian. The romantic half-light shed by the lamp, the chocolate cream and the delectable reading-matter all added up a grand celebration. She angled the light on the folder and unwrapped the chocolate bar. Then, shutting her eyes, she revealed the bill of fare. She counted to ten before opening her eyes again, and her first sight was that of the crown of thorns. She felt a surge of gratitude for the aptness of the symbol. Whatever Brian had prescribed as his specialities lay well and truly within the confines of faith and thus assumed an enviable virtue. She had no need to scruple. The crown of thorns was a plea for her worship and dedication. She had long since ceased to have any religious faith, but now she had discovered a framework for a seemly catechism. She would read the list aloud in solemn and reverent tones, as if it were a prayer.

9

IF MISS HAWKINS THOUGHT THAT SHE WAS THE SOLE DISCIPLE OF Brian's wayward church, she was mistaken, for over the past few days, her high priest had not been idle. He'd been round and about, drumming up business. He had visited the record library in the Town Hall, thinking it would provide a profitable quarry, and as it turned out he was right. From the generous sprinkling of middle-aged ladies, it seemed as if music vied with cats and dogs as the indispensable companion to a loner. He had been there only a few minutes when one of the women actually accosted him. "D'you like music?" she asked, but it was clear from her tone and facial expression that her curiosity about his musicology was minimal. Hers was a cultural form of soliciting. Nevertheless he took the question at its face-value and answered that he did indeed like music and found it a boon companion to one who lived alone, thus making his tastes and his domestic situation immediately clear. The lady, too, had no desire to beat about the bush. "I live alone, too," she said, "perhaps we can listen together sometime?" Her boldness somewhat astonished him, as did his easy lie about his hermit existence. With very little encouragement he had managed either to bury his mother or to establish her at The Petunias, and he was glad that he could do it with so little scruple.

"Come to my place," she was saying, and he noticed how her voice was suddenly a whisper. "I've got some very special lines." She winked at him. Instinctively he moved away, then regretted it, for though he wanted none of her services, he would have given his eye-teeth to see her price-list. It disturbed him to be confronted with the fact that others were in the business, and so brazenly. He reckoned that there were few men in the trade, and they surely had more subtle ways of client-pulling. He heard the patter of her receding footsteps on the parquet floor, and he turned to watch her, as, record-less, she left the room. Her feet and ankles, he noticed, were swollen, and they were stuffed into short-laced boots with precariously high heels. Her feet were the mark of her calling, the sum of a million to-and-fro steps on pavement stones and cobbled alleys, and now, with the illegality of her calling, the respectable parquet floors of the establishment. She did not look back. There could be no regrets attached to her trade, else it would have reminded her that she was a woman withal, and without in any way connecting her pursuit with his, Brian felt faintly sorry for her.

On the way home he decided to do his supermarket shopping. This was normally a Monday occupation, but since he would be otherwise engaged, he would do it forthwith, and his mother, without mentioning it, would appreciate his far-sightedness. He would buy her a bar of chocolate as well. Brian had always done the household shopping and cooking. His mother had always frowned upon domesticity, thinking she was above it, though for what reason Brian never knew, for apart from her reading of thrillers over and over again, she did little else with her time. And she loved to eat and watch television. Since the onset of her condition, she rarely risked going out, though she would oblige Brian to take her for a short walk sometimes for a lungful of fresh air to which she was not overpartial, but she feared the results of its deprivation. Yes, it surely was time she went into care, Brian thought, but for both of them the Twilight Home was out of the question. He wondered often why he hated it so; other old people found it adequate enough. What was so special about his mother that both of them considered it below her station? He had to conclude that there was nothing special at all, but that he could not bring himself to dump her there. When their neighbours had suggested it, he wondered at his stubborn refusal. It wasn't even that he liked his mother, but he disliked her so much that he wanted to give her no cause to blame him, no stage for her masochistic triumph. She said often enough, and often without cause, "You'd like to see me dead, wouldn't you?" Yes, he would, indeed he would, when her moaning would be silenced once and for all. But from the Twilight Home she would bleat out her weary martyrdom and would give him little pleasure. The Petunias was the only solution. There she would not only be out of the way, but grateful for it. He had to find some more clients. The record library had proved infertile ground. He must seek fresh fields. He took a wire trolley and entered the super-market.

He knew its lay-out intimately, for ever since it had opened he had been a regular weekly customer. His needs and his mother's were straightforward and constant. Indeed they were often similar, a thought which often displeased him. So he would move from dairy to fruit, from meat to vegetables, with speed and precision. It was only at the household counter that he dallied, trying to save on the cleaning materials, mops and disinfectants that his mother's condition constantly required. It was as he approached this section of the supermarket that a sense of shame always overcame him, the embarrassment of being seen to have anything to do with women's work. He sampled the prices of the aerosol clean-airs from a dis-tance, feigning only the cursory interest of one who is marginally curious as to how women get through their housekeeping allow-ance. Then, having fixed on the cheapest and largest, he looked furtively around him and dropped the can into his trolley as he was passing by. As he walked he concealed it beneath the frozen chicken, for he regarded it as the most shameful of his purchases. Then followed the need for toilet paper further down the counter. He balked again. Such natural functions were unavoidable, but there was no need to display their necessity in such a public place, and when he saw others collecting their rolls, he could not help but look upon them with a certain disdain, and he was loathe to join their number. The rolls were at the very end of the shelf directly around the counter from the marmalade. He stretched out his hand for a double lavender, which seemed from his distant scrutiny to be the best buy, and as he picked it up from the shelf, another hand, fresh from jam-collecting, reached round the corner for its natural need. Their grasp was simultaneous and on the same double roll, so it was inevitable that one should give way to the other, a sacrifice that Brian was all too ready to make, anything to avoid a confrontation at such a compromising counter. But the face attached to the groping hand now cornered, and was staring at him and meekly thanking him, crumbling with the embarrassment of his discovery of her human frailty. He avoided her gratitude and quickly moved away, paper-less but proud, and with a distinct feeling of gross superiority. He finished his shopping and joined the short queue at the cashier's desk. He was too engrossed in his feeling of separateness to notice the lavender roll on top of the basket of the client in front of him. When he did, he noted, too, the other contents of her trolley. A half pound of butter, one lamb chop, a small piece of cheese, a quarter of tea and a pound of sugar. To clinch it all was a tin of cat food. It was clearly the sum total of provisions of a woman who lived alone. He tried to recall her apologetic face, but he'd given it only a fleeting glance and nothing had registered. So he studied the back of her as if to find some clue to a possible interest in his price-list. The queue moved forward, and she arranged her frugal needs on the counter. She turned to replace the trolley and caught sight of him and gave him again that apologetic smile. He felt he ought to say that she shouldn't worry. He fully understood that like everybody else, or almost everybody else, she, too, had needs which she would have preferred to conceal, but what then was it doing so boldly displayed on the counter? He felt like offering his jacket as a cover. "Isn't it a lovely day?" he said, echoing Miss Hawkins' first introduction. He suddenly felt a strange fondness for Miss Hawkins. No matter how large his clientèle, she would always be his favourite, for it was she, as well as his mother, who both unawares had first put him in business. He would give Miss Hawkins the odd perk or two, he decided.

"Yes, it is, isn't it?" the lavender lady obliged as she filled her shopping-bag with her needs. Her ready agreement was a conversation-stopper, and he scratched in his mind to reopen it.

"Nice day for a walk," he said.

She took it as an invitation, and immediately rejected it. "I have to go home and feed my cat," she said.

He was surprised at her interpretation. He hadn't meant it as an open invitation, and if he had, but he was positive he hadn't, he was a little irritated at having been so summarily dismissed. He felt the need for a come-back. "I wasn't thinking of it for myself," he said. "It was a general remark. I meant other people."

"But we *are* other people," she said, putting him firmly in his place as part of the large, indefinable herd.

He could think of no answer. He should have let it go at that, but he was conscious of a sudden need for revenge, to put this woman in her rightful place, that of servitude. She would make an ideal client. He noticed that she hovered at the end of the counter, feigning some difficulty in arranging her purchases in her bag. Brian concluded that she was waiting for him, and he packed and paid for his purchases quickly, so that by the time he was finished, she, too, was ready to move away. He dangled by her side and out of the shop.

"I go this way," she said, pointing to her left.

"So do I," Brian said, though his disinfected home lay in the other direction. They walked side by side silently.

"Shall I carry your bag?" Brian said after a while.

"That's very kind of you," she said, passing it to him.

He was surprised at how heavy it was, considering the meanness of her shopping. He peeped inside, and underneath the supermarket items, he caught sight of a large box of chocolates. Yes, he decided, she definitely lived alone.

They turned the corner at the end of the supermarket block and into a tree-lined street that was suddenly strangely quiet given its proximity to the High Street traffic. Half-way down the street she stopped. "This is where I live," she said.

He offered her the shopping-bag.

"Would you like a cup of tea?" she said. "Because you carried it," she added quickly, fearing lest the invitation was for its own sake and not by way of recompense.

"I would have carried it anyway," he said. "But I never say no to a cup of tea."

She opened the front door. He noticed a man's umbrella stuck in the hall-stand. The sight upset his calculations, and he thought he might ask her if he could use her bathroom, which was a reliable location to access the gender of occupancy. Once there, he was glad to notice the single toothbrush in the stand, a row of female appliances, and not a male trapping in sight. On the way down-stairs, he peeped into open doorways, and noted two overfurnished bedrooms and a store-room. It was obviously a home of many years' standing. In the sitting-room, the furniture was highly pol-ished, but scratched and scuffed from many years of function. The chair-covers were clean, but frayed and faded, and he had the im-pression that it had once been a family house, a nest from which the birds had flown. And as if echoing his thoughts, she said, "I've lived in this house for forty years. Brought up my children here. They're in Canada now."

"And your husband?"

"I'm a widow," she said. "This fourteen years. Now make yourself comfortable. I'll put the kettle on."

He took advantage of her absence to examine the room for fur-ther clues to her standing. On the sideboard was a line of framed photographs, two of weddings, which he presumed were those of her children. At the far end was a silver-framed portrait of a middle-aged man in army officer's uniform. Presumably the dear departed. In the corner was a revolving book-case, containing more magazines than books, but among the latter he noticed a pre-ponderance of titles pertaining to spiritualism and the life hereafter. He made a note to incorporate that subject into his sales patter. He heard the squeak of a tea-trolley and took his seat again. Her tea-service, he noticed, was the same that his mother had had for many years. It was a blue willow-pattern and had probably been bought around the same time, for nowadays he knew that such china was very expensive. His mother rarely ordered its use. It was the best china, she kept telling him, and kept for visitors, but since visitors were rare, the set gathered cobwebs on the top shelf of the pantry. He was glad she had the same set. He felt himself part of a special occasion. She poured the tea.

"Your husband?" he said, nodding in the direction of the photograph.

"Yes, that's George. That photograph was taken only a week before he died. A regimental dinner, it was. He was a regular soldier, you see."

"He looks a very interesting gentleman," Brian said, hoping with this observation to tempt her into revealing more of her husband's nature, so that he could gauge whether or not he was wasting his time.

"He was indeed," she said, "though he had his little quirks."

Brian's hopes rose. "Quirks?"

"Well, he was a stickler for tidiness. Everything had to be in apple-pie order, like soldiers in line. I've seen him get up from his armchair, for the express purpose of adjusting one cushion that was a millimetre out of place."

Sick enough, Brian thought, and very promising. "How did you deal with all that?" he said.

"I let it be," she said, " 'cos I have my little quirks, too."

It was acceptable to discuss the idiosyncrasies of the dead. It was altogether too personal to show curiosity about those of the living and practising. And though he itched to know what her quirks were, he made a point of not enquiring further. There was a silence between them that timed his unasked question, and her reticence to go any further.

"What's your name," he said, "if you don't mind my asking?"

"Violet," she said. "Violet Makins. And yours?"

He hesitated, needing to search for one. He was aware that his trade was illicit, and that he must have an alibi in the event of discovery.

"Felix," he said. "It's a silly name, I know," he added, playing for time to think of an appropriate handle. "Hawkins," he said suddenly. "Felix Hawkins." His first, and so far only, client would have been flattered.

"Are you a retired man?" she said. She framed the question in such a way as to place him in a specific class, to give him a status. Had she simply asked if he had retired, it might have hinted at his old age or possibly failure.

"No," he said, "I have a little business."

"Oh, yes," she said, and waited for him to elaborate.

"I sell services," he said.

"That's interesting," Mrs. Makins said politely. "What sort of services?"

"My own," he said.

"I don't quite understand you."

What the hell, he thought, he need never see her again if he didn't so choose, and it was worth a try in the hope of a new client. But even though he was prepared to be totally honest, he couldn't find words to explain the nature of his trade. He wasn't really selling anything, because even after he had sold it, he still had it, like any respectable call-girl. "It's hard to explain," he said. "It's—well, if you want anything, I'll sell it to you."

"Such as?" she said.

Then he was stuck again, reluctant to spell out particulars. "Well," he said, "let me put it this way. I only deal with women."

They both listened to the shattering silence that ensued. Then Brian quickly finished his tea in case she should show him the door.

"That's very interesting," Mrs. Makins said softly, and from the tone of her voice she was clearly more than interested. "Would you like some more tea?" she said.

He passed her his cup, and as she poured, she said, "I've never met anyone in your trade before."

"Oh, there are hundreds of us," Brian said, hoping that quantity was a guarantee of legality. "I know at least half a dozen personally."

"But how do you get your clients?" she said.

Brian noticed that her accent was suddenly very upper class, as if to give official license to a vocation that, looked squarely in its common face, was downright salacious. She indicated without doubt a personal interest in the goods he had for sale, and she was anxious, for her own sake, to give them class.

Brian munched happily on a second piece of cake. "I meet them quite by accident," he said, and then added, at only a small risk, "rather as I met you."

She laughed, a gay, little, aristocratic tinkle, and Brian began to have some idea of what her little quirks were.

"D'you have a list of services?" she said.

The woman cottoned on very quickly, and Brian hardly knew his luck. He put his hand inside his inside pocket, and drew out a folded parchment. This one he had decorated with houses and all signs of habitation, indicating some domestic security on the services rendered. Brazenly he handed it over. She took a pair of glasses and held them over her eyes. She refused to fix them firmly on her ears, holding them all the time, as if to give him the impression that glasses were only a very occasional need of hers and not permanent enough to warrant fixture. He watched her as she read. Occasionally she let out a well-born sigh or a courtly giggle. Brian began to calculate his income with confidence. She read the list to the end, and by the angle of her lowered eyes, she was clearly reading the more expensive services with interest and relish. "May I keep this?" she said.

"Are you interested?"

"Certainly," she said. "But are you discreet?"

"I wish I could name some of my satisfied clients," he said, "but secrecy must be part of such a service." He sighed, well satisfied with himself.

"Well, in that case, I am interested," she said. "With the smaller services," she added quickly. "I don't know how many of the others I shall need." She took in a quick and genteel breath, regretting perhaps that she had been so forward. "Shall I clear away the tea-things," she said, "and then we can start? I'll draw the curtains if you don't mind."

Suddenly Brian did mind very much. He was not prepared for her eagerness, and besides he had no notion of what to do. He'd had so little practice. He tried to reason with himself that this was as good a time as any to start, but he was too nervous to take the sudden plunge. "I'd love to," he said, "but I do have a client this afternoon and she lives quite a long way away." He saw the disappointment on her face. "I'm sorry," he said, "but we could make another time." He took out his diary and opened it furtively, trying to hide from her its emptiness. "What about tomorrow," he said, "round about this time? I could give you as long as you require." He was happy with his choice of word. Services were not wanted: such a word hinted at lust. They were required, they were needed to keep the wheels of whatever it was smoothly turning.

"Tomorrow would do very nicely," she said. She took him to the door. "I wonder," she said, as he was leaving, "would you mind very much if tomorrow you came and went by the back entrance? You understand," she said. "In case it will be regular, the neighbours will be very curious."

"Of course," he said. "I would have done that in any case."

"Ta-ta then," she said, her accent suddenly slipping. "Till tomorrow."

He closed the gate after him and walked briskly down the road, needing to prove his hurry in case she was watching him through the window. He was already regretting that he hadn't served her there and then, fearing perhaps that by the morning she might have second and more respectable thoughts. And what guarantee did he have that he could function at all? He needed practice, and above all confidence, which could only be fed by a client's satisfaction. For a moment he thought of going back to Violet, claiming that he'd made a mistake with the day of his appointment. But that would give an impression of non-professionalism which could certainly go hand in hand with indiscretion. And he had his goodwill to maintain. No, he would go straight home and sit quietly in his bedroom and think carefully how to handle the trade he'd been landed with. He concluded that for a man of enterprise it was indeed an easy and profitable calling, and he wondered whether indeed there were as many in the profession as he had sworn to Mrs. Makins.

When he got home, he unpacked his shopping.

"Are you back then?" his mother said, staring at him and seething with neglect.

He looked with disgust at the puddle at her feet, while she looked at it with pleasure, as if she'd kept a promise she'd made to herself when he went out. The need to get rid of her was becoming almost an obsession with him. He was glad he had other things to contemplate, for he was encouraged by his day's sortie, but still fearful of his own ability to capitalize on it. He looked at his mother with abject loathing.

"It's all your fault," he shouted at her, and she, understanding the fault to be the puddle, welcomed his angry irritation, promising herself to repeat the performance each one of his working afternoons. It only took two extra glasses of water to perform, a small inconvenience for such a rich pay-off. He went into the kitchen for the mop, and leaning on it, he calculated his possible turn-over. Two more clients like Mrs. Makins, and all of them wanting his whole range of services, could clinch the Petunias for as long as the old bitch survived. The thought cheered him, and he went back to the sitting-room. "Well, you can't help it, can you, my dear?" he said, placing his hand on her knee.

His sudden kindness threw her, and gave her little reason for further battle. "You'll be glad when I'm gone, though, won't you?" she said, hanging on for dear life to the frayed remnant of their bickering.

"What will I do without you?" he said, as he always said. That was his signature on the truce, whether she liked it or not. She watched him mop the floor, and she tried to reap some satisfaction from that. But his irritation had clearly evaporated. "I bought you some chocolate," he said. It was his final declaration of armistice, and her watering mouth disarmed her.

10

BY MONDAY, MISS HAWKINS' SCARF HAD ANGERED ANOTHER foot and a half. The more aware she became of the new and exciting turn in her life, the more she cursed its long delay. Now her mind was continuously filled with Orphanage thoughts and the blight that Matron had scarred her with. So she knitted and knitted, and as she plained away, she read and re-read Brian's bill of fare, and set to knitting again. But on this Monday morning she folded it neatly away because she had other things to do. She was going to bake Brian a cake, and lay the tea-table with infinite care. She had bought a bottle of cheap port, thinking that she might need a tonic for her failing courage. Brian was new at the game, too, so he, too, might be grateful for a stiffener. She set the bottle and two glasses discreetly at the side. When she was ready, the morning was still young and she was faced with the daily task of the diary's order. Although the day was likely to be eventful enough, and with enough data for a formal diarist to be proud of, she could not help but regard the diary as a book of challenges. That was how it had begun, with the small and timid order to forage for survival. The tone of its commands had changed. They had become more daring, and she was determined to maintain the high standards of risk that she set herself. But to-day presented a problem. What she had committed herself to do was daring enough, and to inscribe simply "Acquitted myself" would have been challenge enough. But she needed something even more reckless to honour the diary's purpose.

She looked again at Brian's list, and for the hundredth time totted up the prices of the first service section. If she were to treat herself to each one of them, her total investment would be a little over £2. For in her mind there was no doubt that it was an investment, unorthodox, she knew, but a way, and a pleasant one, Brian had assured her, of putting something by. The investment itself, according to Brian's promises, carried little risk, but not enough for Miss Hawkins, who by now had become intrepid enough to flaunt the minimal chance. She was becoming more and more daring, tempted each day to the margins of the impossible. A £2 investment was clearly more than she could afford, but not more enough for daring. She would invest double, she decided, even if it meant overlapping into the second service section, which she blushed to read, leave alone imagine herself as recipient. So she opened her diary to the current page, and inscribed, "Brian came to tea. I spent four pounds." She locked the book with the golden key and hid it on the larder shelf.

She started to make preparations for their rendezvous. She loaded the tea-trolley with her best china, a dish of assorted biscuits and the freshly baked cake. She had second thoughts about the bottle of port and decided that on the side-table it looked too exposed, so she hid it with the glasses on the lower level of the trolley. She didn't want Brian to think she had bought it expressly for their first business exchange, so she opened it and poured herself a generous helping which she sipped in the course of making her other arrangements. She wheeled the trolley into the sitting-room and put on all the lights, then she drew the curtains, shutting out the morning sun. She picked Maurice off the wall, and with a whispered apology for disturbing him, she took him into the bedroom and hid his faceless moustache under the bed. Back in the sitting-room, she took the list and propped it open on the mantelpiece, facing the settee, where she presumed the business would operate. She sat down and judged the distance from the mantelpiece for easy reading and for a need to keep a check on her spending. She adjusted the settee until her vision was perfect, then she moved over to the door to take in a master-view of the room. It looked very romantic, she decided, conducive to the business in hand. She took another sip of port to give herself courage for the encounter, for she had to admit to a growing nervousness, and she wished he would come quickly so that she could get it over with and tick off the order in her little book. She opened her handbag and checked on her change. Her money, all four pounds of it, was in small denominations. She intended to pay as she bought. She had gone to the bank especially for the purpose of changing the notes, otherwise Brian, lacking the right change, might have talked her into the idea of hire-purchase, and it was a principle with her never to buy anything that you couldn't pay for on the nail. She stacked the money in neat little piles on the small table next to the settee. She intended to sit on that side, so that payment would be discreet and handy.

By lunchtime, Miss Hawkins' preparations were complete. She had bathed and put on her best dress, but she had retained her slippers to offset the formality of her appearance and to give the casual air of the ordinary to an extraordinary event. In small and nervous sips, she had managed to down half the bottle of port, and she felt aglow. Her erstwhile nervousness now focused only on whether her home-baked sponge was up to standard. And to settle that small anxiety, she cut herself a small slice, dunking it in her port, and found it satisfactory. There was nothing more to do now except to wait for him. She sat down on her side of the settee, and read off the items in the first and second sections, slowly and carefully, as if her eyes were being tested on an optician's chart. The final section of Brian's services was concealed under the fold. She would not be needing those services today, certainly not today, and probably never. Never, never, she said to herself. Even if she had an appetite for them, they were certainly beyond her means, so costly, indeed, that they were hardly worth bargaining for, for even at half their price she could not afford them. Yet she had to admit they made very exciting reading. She took the folder from the mantelpiece and revealed the category of unattainables.

She snuggled into the corner-angle of uncut moquette and read them aloud. There was a gradual build-up of services and prices, and the final offer, the most, she assumed, Brian or any of his kind was capable of serving, was charged at the princely sum of £50. The reading of the service thrilled her almost beyond control. Its outrageous fee fed her excitement, and she saw through her woollen slippers the frenetic movement of her wiggling toes. She wished that he would come. She read the section over again, trying to convince herself that the reading of it was enough, and praying that it would always be enough and that she should never seek to translate it into practical terms, even if Brian were to give it her for nothing. But above all she prayed that her diary would never order her to it. Miss Hawkins had long ago dispensed with God in any religious form, but she still clung to the estates of heaven and hell, and there was no doubt in her orphan-washed mind that non-virgins, if unmarried, went straight to the fire without any right of appeal. Without using any of the words, Matron had always made that very clear. She remembered the special talk Matron gave to the small cluster of girls as they left for their first working-day at the For Your Pleasure factory. They were all highly excited. The prospect of freedom, with the added bonus of unlimited sweets, was intoxicating, and it was difficult to concentrate on the final words of wisdom and warning with which Matron burdened her departing wards. Although they were now free of her, and need never in the whole of their lives look upon her angry face again, she had so conditioned them to fear that they trembled even on the brink of their parole, and listened, as they had always listened to her sour words of hate, mistrust and hell-fire warnings. "Never forget what you came from," she told them. "What you came from is nothing and that is easy to remember. You have no fathers, and your mothers don't count, for they are fallen women, fallen in the sight of God."

"She's not," Hawkins protested, though she'd never seen her mother or even heard her name. "My mother was a good woman," she said, with the courage of a school-leaver.

Matron was regretfully aware that the bread and water days were over. All she could do was to spit in Hawkins' direction. "I can see the way you're going, Hawkins. You'll end up like your mother, on the streets, riddled with disease and poverty. But the rest of you girls," she said, turning her back on Hawkins, "there's hope for you. I want you to take my advice," and Hawkins saw a red flush on the back of her starched neck. "Whenever you meet a man," she said quickly, "cross your legs, and keep them crossed until you've left the altar. Or I promise you that you will go to the fire and burn for ever after, Amen." The girls shuddered, and though the words were not addressed to her, so did Hawkins, and on no-one did the words have a more lasting effect, for throughout her confectioned life, under the bench, the desk, and finally the till, she had kept her legs firmly locked.

Miss Hawkins looked at them now, and saw the frightened reef-knot of her ankles and she stiffened with fear and fury. Quickly she reached for her knitting and plained Matron away in a spleen of olive green. It took almost six inches for her anger to evaporate, and it was time for Brian's visit. She put the knitting away and took a generous gulp of port.

When the door-bell rang, she unfastened her extremities and straightened her best dress. She waited until he rang a second time. Her blushes and tremblings proclaimed her eagerness enough, without her having to rush to the door. On the second ring, she went slowly through the hall, assuming a look of wonder on her face as to who it was, and for what reason anyone should call on her. And it was a questioning look of surprise that Brian countered as he stood at the door twiddling with his hat.

"Hullo," he said, and there was no shyness in him. His manner was abrupt and business-like. "May I come in?" he said briskly, as if there were no time to lose. As if he had another client waiting. Which indeed he had, in the person of Violet Makins' friend to whom he had been fulsomely recommended. His first transaction with Violet had been an unparalleled success. She had concentrated on the first and second sections of his bill of fare, and it was clear to Brian that given time she would make her lustful way through the whole meal. Her appetite, even for the hors d'oeuvres, was gargantuan, and so satisfied was she that she immediately gave him the name of her friend, to whom she had confided the details of Brian's servicing, and who had shown more than average interest in becoming a client. Mrs. Makins had indicated that he could do for her twice a week, and her friend, no doubt, would want likewise. He looked forward to a discreet accumulation of clients and goodwill, and if his strength were overtaxed, why, he might even go into discreet partnership. He looked at Miss Hawkins, and though he felt instinctively that the lady was not a great spender, he nevertheless felt a strong affection for her. Although he'd been in business for less than a week, he already knew how to recognize innocence, and dear Miss Hawkins was shrivelled with it. He followed her into the sitting-room.

"I'll put the kettle on," she said, rushing out again, unwilling to bear witness to his reactions to all her ceremonials, the drawn curtains, the port and the up-stage placing of the settee.

Brian sat down and was pleased with the setting. The desperate void on the top of the port-bottle moved him infinitely, and he decided to throw in one or two services for nothing. A fact that would not have pleased Miss Hawkins had she known of his intended generosity, for she was in duty bound to spend £4 on her investment without availing herself of the more costly services. She poured the hot water on the tea-leaves, and waited while it infused, shifting from one foot to the other, dreading the brewed moment when there could no longer be any delay. Yet at the same time, she was anxious to get on with it, if only to speed the pleasure of ticking off her diary's order. She took the tea-pot into the sitting-room. "Nice little place you've got here," he said. He liked Violet's sitting-room better. Somehow with its old pieces of silver, and framed family photographs, it had more substance. It spoke of a past that had been eventful, it spoke softly of inheritance and continuity. Miss Hawkins' sitting-room was barren and unsired. It spoke of no dowry and of no bequest. It was here for the length of her lifetime, and afterwards it would be re-papered without respect or regret.

"It's very comfortable for one person," Miss Hawkins said. She thought of Maurice under the bed and had a sudden thrilling notion of adultery. "D'you take sugar?"

He shook his head. "I'm sweet enough," he said.

"But you'll have some cake," she said, cutting him a slice. The tea and all that attended it was part of the ritual of postponement, and it was clearly more for the hostess's sake than that of her guest. Brian was already practised enough in his trade to dispense with the preamble trimmings. "Come and sit down," he said, patting the moquette beside him. Then for the first time he noticed the neat pile of change on the table. He totted it up quickly with his eye, and was rather surprised by her intended extravagance. He girded his aging loins. She settled herself by his side, her legs demurely crossed at the ankle.

"You're looking very lovely in that frock," he said. Flirting was for free, and he'd learned it as a useful prelude to the serious part of the business.

"Thank you ever so much," she said, grateful that he still saw the woman in her, and not solely a paying recipient of his trade.

"Have you decided what you want?" he said, putting his cup of tea on one side. She was surprised by his promptness and his determination to get things going.

"I'd like some port," she said faint-heartedly, and without unlocking her legs, she reached over for the bottle. "Would you like a drop?"

"I think I can manage with just the tea," he said.

"Oh, I don't *need* it," she said quickly, and she wondered why he was pulling rank on her. "You haven't done this sort of thing before?" she asked, needing to reassure herself that there was a mutual innocence abroad.

"Of course not," he said, recalling the useful lessons that Violet had taught him. "I just don't like port very much. It's a lady's drink," he said, "so you enjoy it."

She obeyed and took a generous mouthful. Then when it was down, and she was re-settled, locked in the settee, there was no longer any earthly reason why they shouldn't get down to business.

"I thought I'd try the first section," she said. "I've added it all up and it comes to one pound. And I'd like to pay you in advance," she said. She took one pile of the change and gave it to him. He did not count it, for he had already gauged its worth from his place on the settee, and he put it in his trouser-pocket. "Would you like the lights out?" he said. Violet had been prepared to spend far more money in the dark, for she'd been altogether more comfortable as a non-eyewitness.

Miss Hawkins was grateful for his consideration. "I'll do it," she said, getting up. "I can feel my way around." She turned off all the lights, and crossed over to the curtains, and closed off the small chinks of sunlight from outside. Now it was totally dark and she had to grope her way back to the settee. She tumbled down close beside him, and she was able to use the dark as an excuse for her unseemly lack of decorum. Then she realized that she could no longer see the bill of fare that stood open on the mantelpiece.

"Now I can't see the bill," she said.

"Don't worry," he said, "I know it by heart."

"So do I, I suppose," she giggled.

"We'll start at the beginning and we'll go right through."

"Just the first section," she added, on her guard. "Then we'll see."

"Oh, we'll see alright," Brian said, "and we *won't* see either, shall we?"

She was prepared to leave it at that.

He took her hand, but not as he had taken it before, as a teasing sample of his services. This time he took each part of it, as Violet had guided him, alternating the parts with the whole, stroking and pressing, and occasionally pressing so hard, especially in the palm, that it almost hurt. It was the hurting that Miss Hawkins liked best, and she was prepared to pay over and over again to test the threshold of her acceptance of his cruelty. Thus he went through each item in a teasing manner, and when she paid for a repeat performance, given the limitations of the target, he really gave his all. In the second performance, Miss Hawkins felt urgent stirrings in those parts of her body that were catered for only in the forbidden section, and she had to call a halt for a while, a breathing space, as she told Brian, for she still had half her bounden money to spend. She persuaded him to a thimbleful of port, but refrained herself.

She needed no more stimulant, or her nest-egg would be scrambled in one fell swoop. She moved away from him on the couch and was horrified to notice that, somewhere along the line, her ankles had freed their lock, and she thought of Matron and her promise of eternal damnation. Yet she had only spent £2, hardly enough for a mild reprimand. Eternal damnation, if it proved to be worth it, would surely cost a lot more. She promised herself that she would never go that far, and she moved closer to Brian so that his encore would prove her sworn limitations.

She handed over the third pile, and coyly suggested they move onto the second section of the catalogue. Brian, sensing that she would want a repeat of this section as well, and mindful of his later engagement, covered the items in quick succession, and the speed of it, contrary to all expectations, laced it with even greater thrills. "More, more," she squealed, handing over the last pile, and he repeated it, slower this time, because he didn't want to overcheat her. When he'd run it through a second time, Brian said, "That's all for today. I have to get back to my mother. I hope you're satisfied."

Miss Hawkins looked again at her wayward loose ankles. And she resolved that the next time Brian came to serve her, she would tie them together with string. Indeed, Brian himself could tie them, very tightly, she would insist, so that it would hurt her splendidly, and Brian, without knowing, would be giving an extra service for nothing.

"Yes, I'm very satisfied," she said, getting up. "Can you come again next Monday?"

"I'll be glad," he said. "I rather enjoy it, don't you?" He had to remind himself that he, too, was supposed to be new at the game, so he chorused her innocent giggling. "It's going to get better and better," he promised.

"It's a lovely way of saving," Miss Hawkins said. "You'll keep the accounts, will you?" she said.

"Don't you worry, Jean," he reassured her, and his calling her by name was more reassurance than she could ever hope for.

She saw him to the door and the front gate, and waved to him as he hurried down the street. The back-door syndrome of Mrs. Violet Makins had no place in Miss Hawkins' production. She had no shame of what had passed in her sitting-room. The last hour or so had been by way of a tea-time confessional, and even Matron had granted that confession was good for the soul. She shut the front door behind her and returned to her sanctuary. She sat in the darkened room reliving her wild purchases. She had intended having Maurice to dinner, but suddenly she didn't want to tell him of the day's events. She didn't want to share them with anybody, partly for the sake of her own privacy, and partly out of sheer exhaustion. She decided to go to bed early and read her way into a romantic sleep. But first there was the joy of ticking. She unlocked her diary and opened it to the day's order. She had spent the required sum and it had been more than she could afford. She ticked it off with acute pleasure. Then she cleared the tea-trolley and drew the blinds open to release the fading light of day. She undressed slowly and gently and, as always, with her eyes tightly closed, but treating her unseen body with a new and tender care. Then she snuggled with her novelette between the sheets, while the faceless Maurice lay cuckold under the bed.

II

11

MISS HAWKINS' DIARY WAS THREE YEARS OLD. SHE FLICKED through the thousand-odd pages, and found them blood-red with obedience. She had dutifully served more than half her sentence. Only occasionally did she wonder what she would do with her official freedom when the time came. She avoided giving it much thought, because in the beginning, the diary had been but a postponement of a self-inflicted quietus, and it was logical that once it was obsolete, she was free to carry out her original intention. But she no longer had any appetite for that manoeuvre. Her life had become meaningful in the pursuit of pleasure. She had no scruple about enjoying herself. There was no sin in loving and believing oneself loved, and her weekly sitting-room activities became more and more a ritual of worship, and Brian her constant priest. But if she chose to go on living after her sentence had expired, she did sometimes wonder how it would be possible without the diary. It was true that sometimes she loathed her little order book and feared it as it colonized her more and more. Yet without it, she would feel herself disoriented. She could, of course, buy a second five-year round, but there would have been something artificial about obedience if it were to her own prescribed orders. As far as she was concerned, her present diary was itself an order from others, from all her previous masters, and all she had to do was obey.

Such were Miss Hawkins' thoughts on this New Year's Day of the fourth year of her sentence. It was time for stock-taking and sorting out her accounts. She had been putting it off for a long time. Over the past three years she had donated over a thousand pounds to Brian's church, and during that time she had not sampled even one item of his final category. In that respect she had been more moral than thrifty, for even to read that section was to kindle the purgatorial fire. She had to add to all that the weekly expense of a rich, home-baked cake and a bottle of port. There was also a weekly expenditure on candles. After their first few sitting-room sessions, it was Brian who had suggested a little light on the proceedings. He wanted to see what he was doing to ensure that, as far as the required service was concerned, he was not out of bounds, for the difference between a favour of one price, and another that cost double, was a difference of only one finger. Nothing was for nothing. But for Miss Hawkins, the candles shed a flattering and romantic light on the proceedings, as well as underlining the sense of tabernacle. Her wool budget, too, was astronomical, for though her life was reliably punctuated with pleasure, her intermittent anger never abated, and the scarf was now some forty yards long. Miss Hawkins had cause for concern, and it was time for her to set down her columns of Income and Expenditure. The former was constant, consisting of her gratuity, pension and the interest on her shrinking nest-egg. It was that particular that worried her. She wondered how Brian had invested her savings, and what he was doing with its returns. He never volunteered information, and she would have thought that an investment of one thousand pounds would have given him something to talk about, some progress report to enlighten her. When she herself mentioned it from time to time, he assured her with a smile that all was well. So she had no idea of how poor or how rich she was. Over the last three years she had occasionally and obliquely mentioned marriage, not necessarily as a state specific to herself, but as a notion in general. Brian had never expressed any opposition. Indeed he saw it as something to be striven for, and once even he had mentioned the possibility of the two of them joining hands without any payment in advance. She was wary of nagging him about her savings in case he really did intend to use them for their nuptials, and she did not want to risk the possibility that he would change his mind. So from time to time she fretted and feared, and hated herself as well as Brian. And all the accumulated knots of anger and bitterness she unravelled in her knitting.

She put the diary aside and gave up any further attempt at stock-taking. She had to face the fact that she had insufficient data. She looked at her watch. Soon it would be opening time at the Pirate's Arms. Over the years she had become one of its regulars. She had a table in the corner of the private bar, which was understood by other regulars to be Miss Hawkins' reserve. On the table she would spread her handbag, a book or sometimes, if the plaining mood were upon her, her knitting. The interminable scarf had become a topic of conversation at the pub, and for some was a proof of Miss Hawkins' eccentricity. And though they knew nothing about her, they warmed to her. They asked her no questions, because she gave off a very clear signal of privacy. Miss Hawkins looked forward to her daily tipple, taken usually in the early evening, but this morning's drink was a bonus, since it marked the beginning of a new year, a year, she dared to hope, which would see the changing of her name. As she sat there sipping her gin and lime, an observer would have seen her give a sudden start, and noticed that her face had turned an ashen grey. For Miss Hawkins had just remembered that, on leaving the house, she had forgotten to write out the day's order. In the three years since her sentence was pronounced, she had never once gone out of the door without prescribing some duty. And not any old duty, but one that contained an element of risk. Now all her orders had been Brian-oriented. She had spread her duty-net pretty wide. She had, for example, ordered herself to go swimming in the local baths, though she had never before set foot in a pool. Once her diary had sent her on a dustbin treasure hunt with specific orders as to what to bring home, and that order had sent her foraging late into the night until her list of requirements was complete. Now she was unnerved by her neglect and she began to shiver like an addict deprived of a fix. She downed her gin and lime, noticing that a few clients were watching her, and she got up quickly, saying, "I left the oven on," and she left the pub covered with shame. She hurried home and went straight to the leather-bound tyranny. Each new year started on a piece of parchment paper covered with a wispy tissue. There was a special column headed "New Year Resolutions," and it was one order that she ignored, since she considered that every day contained resolutions that she had obediently carried out. That column was child's play, and too amateur for a hardy professional like herself. She turned over the parchment and smoothed her hand down the virgin new year's page. Its untrodden whiteness called for a dramatic sortie, a brave footprint of a pioneer to an unchartered land. She no longer deliberated on the ease or difficulty of an order's execution. She tended to write down whatever wishful thinking played in her mind, and at this moment, on the first day of the new year, she allowed herself one single resolution. But only because it was in itself an order, which required all her reserves of courage and cunning to fulfil. So she wrote high on the page, and in large capitals, for she was not unmindful of its timing as a turning-point in her life, "MADE ARRANGEMENTS FOR MY WEDDING-DRESS." It was only after she'd written it down that she realized the fulfilment of such an order on New Year's Day, when most of the shops were closed, was well nigh impossible. But it was too late to erase it. Her willingness would have to overcome all obstacles. She buttoned her coat and left the house once more.

She had intended to return to the pub, partly because she fancied an extra gin and lime to celebrate the new year, and because her hasty departure and manufactured excuse inferred a return, and she liked to believe that the regulars would miss her. Moreover, she needed that drink to fortify her for the arduous task the diary had set her. And she would have a cigarette, too, not as a means of postponement, but as an additional stimulant. All her adult life she had been wary of cigarettes, but her new-found taste for alcohol somehow included tobacco. She tried to ration herself for reasons of economy. Her pull to alcohol was stronger, but she was finding it increasingly difficult to drink without a cigarette. Again she thought of her stock-taking, and all its unavailable data. But at least she could be sure of Expenditure, and there seemed to be no reason at all why she shouldn't budget for tobacco. She called in at the news-agent's next door to the Pirate's Arms. There was a small queue, and while she waited she idly read the small ads in the glass case above the stationery counter. She read of rooms to let and washing machines for sale, and an offer of French lessons with the bracketed codicil of "genuine." And beneath this declaration of honest academic intent, a Mrs. Daisy Church offered her services as dress-maker. She had no phone number, but her address was within walking distance of the shop. Miss Hawkins looked upon the notice as a timely deliverance and she repeated the address to herself until she learned it by heart. The salesgirl asked her what she wanted, and still in her diary's order, she answered, "A wedding-dress," and the girl giggled out of pity and embarrassment. The hurt Miss Hawkins giggled, too, for that was the only way of confirming it as a deliberate joke.

"Twenty tipped," she said, "and a Happy New Year."

The girl felt less pity and more embarrassment and quickly she handed over the cigarettes, for such eccentricity gave the shop a bad name. Miss Hawkins lit up immediately. Over the years, since the beginning of her sentence, her discretion had by necessity evaporated. Her day's order was a reckless one, which allowed no room for prudence, and so she might as well in all particulars throw caution to the winds. Between blatant and public puffs on her cigarette, she repeated the address to herself and made her way in that direction.

Mrs. Church tried not to look surprised when Miss Hawkins stated her purpose at her front door. It had been a long time since a client had called. The little notice in the news-agent's was a standing order, and had been there at a small weekly cost for many years. Her clients, such as they were, came by way of recommendation, and were women of uncommon shapes and sizes, for whom off-the-peg did not cater. Mrs. Church sized up Miss Hawkins, and with a practised eye judged her a simple size 14, who would have no problems whatsoever in any chain store. She therefore must want something special, something perhaps that needed privacy to acquire.

She showed her into her work-room. There was a musty smell inside, as if the room had not been used for some time. "I hope you're not in a hurry," Mrs. Church said, sensing her client's wariness. "I've got a lot of work on hand. I'm doing a wedding in three weeks' time," she invented. "Three bridesmaid dresses and one for the bride's mother. Rushed off my feet, I am."

Miss Hawkins relaxed, confident in Mrs. Church's speciality. "I'm not in a desperate hurry," she said; "I'm getting married in six months' time." The date was arbitrary, but she wanted to assure Mrs. Church that she was not rushing her.

"My congratulations," the dressmaker said. "You've been married before, of course?"

"This is my first time," Miss Hawkins said proudly. "Not that I haven't had offers, but I've been very fussy."

Mrs. Church began to feel sorry for her. "What colour are you thinking of, dear?"

Miss Hawkins thought she had been misunderstood. "It's my first time," she said primly, "so naturally I shall want white." Her virgin status was something she was quite ready to flaunt if called upon, because its retention had cost her dear. She knew, of course, that, according to Brian's bill of fare, it would be far more costly to give it away. The temptation had often assaulted her, and she could have found ways and means of raising the cash. So she was proud that she had resisted, and there was no reason why she shouldn't share this pride with Mrs. Church.

"That'll be very nice," the dress-maker said with little enthusiasm. "What style did you have in mind?"

"Have you any patterns?"

Mrs. Church opened a cupboard and took out a pile of books. She put them on the work-table and opened a few at the required nuptial page. Miss Hawkins noted that the books were around ten years old, and Mrs. Church, who had a telepathic knack, hastily assured her that all the old styles had come back into fashion. Miss Hawkins' eye fell on a long white satin creation, with yards of skirt and train, a nipped-in waist and childlike Peter Pan collar. She put her finger on it decisively. "I'd like that one," she said.

Mrs. Church winced. "Don't you think that one would be more suitable?" she said, pointing to a matronly gown suitable for a bride's mother.

"Or that one, or that?" she said. "That one is very becoming." As delicately as possible, she tried to persuade her client that no matter how pure her anatomical status, she was rather too old for cherry-blossom. But Miss Hawkins had made up her mind. "I want that one," she said. "It's my day," as if Mrs. Church were denying her, "and I must look my best."

"Of course. I'll take your measurements."

Miss Hawkins took off her coat and stood to attention. She had never had a dress made before and she was prepared to put herself entirely in Mrs. Church's nuptial hands. As the dress-maker had supposed, she was an exact size 14, and she was relieved that there would be no need for a pattern adjustment. She made a quick and audible sum in her head. "You'll need quite a lot of material, I'm afraid," she said. "The skirt alone is seven yards. Altogether it will be eleven. In a heavy white satin. Should be beautiful." She tried to concentrate on the dress itself, eliminating the model. It could indeed be quite a piece of haute couture.

"What about the net for the head-dress?"

Mrs. Church was quickly brought down to earth, and felt called upon to make a small objection. "Don't you think a simple veil over the hair would be more suitable?"

"I want the tiara."

Mrs. Church began to pity her again, and hoped she would not have to witness the wedding. "That'll be four yards of silk net," she said, "and the crown you'll have to buy separately."

Miss Hawkins was satisfied. "I'll buy the material tomorrow," she said, "and I'll drop it in on my way home. I live close by, so I can come for a fitting at any time."

"It'll be a month yet," Mrs. Church reminded her, suddenly anxious about her rusty sartorial skills.

"That's alright," Miss Hawkins said. "I just like to have everything to hand."

As she put on her coat, Mrs. Church tried to blind herself to the vision of grey mutton clothed in lamb. On the top of Miss Hawkins' head, the cherry-blossom was sprouting. Once again the good lady tried to get her client to change her mind.

"What did you wear when you were a bride?" Miss Hawkins said.

"I wore a dress very like the one you've chosen. But I was eighteen years old."

"Age is in the heart, my dear," Miss Hawkins said. "You had your day, and now I shall have mine."

"What is the groom going to wear?" Mrs. Church dared to ask, and she did not miss the shock on Miss Hawkins' face.

"Top hat and tails," she said after a flinching pause, scraping her memory of an old Fred Astaire movie.

And then Mrs. Church was convinced that there was no groom, nor ever would be, and that the poor woman was going to inordinate and expensive lengths to satisfy a day-dream. She wondered whether she would ever return.

Miss Hawkins reached home and lit another cigarette. She'd had a distinct feeling of unease ever since she'd left the dress-maker's house that was not offset even by the pleasure of ticking off the day's order. Mrs. Church's objection to her choice of style, and her final question about the groom's apparel, had only served to underline her own lack of confidence in the event she was so busily producing. Angrily she reached for her knitting. She puffed furiously at her cigarette, letting it dangle from the corner of her mouth, her one eye closed to avoid the smoke while she knitted out her fury. She recalled the picture of the bride in the fashion book, and without much difficulty was able to translate it to her own person. This made her feel a lot better, and she looked forward to buying the material on the following day. She convinced herself that she would marry in June, a suitable month for such a ceremony, and she did not doubt that by then her diary would be prepared to order her to the altar. She wondered how and where they would settle. She didn't particularly like Brian's house. She much preferred her own. She poured herself a little port, and holding the glass in her hand, she went from room to room, and in her mind she rearranged her dwelling to accommodate a husband. She stood at the bedroom door. It already housed a double bed, and she shivered with excitement when she gave a thought to its new and unknown duties. The wardrobe was small, but there was room enough along the same wall for a second. He would have to share her dressing-table, she decided, as well as the chest of drawers. He could have the two bottom drawers and she set to work immediately emptying his share of space. In half an hour she had changed the room into a marriage-chamber, and she marvelled at the easy readjustment. The kitchen was her own domain, and needed no change. Neither did the sitting-room, she decided, unless he wanted to bring some things of his own. She had a spare room with a small single bed, and this would be used when occasionally they might need a rest from each other. Miss Hawkins assured herself that the best marriages needed the occasional respite. Yes, she decided, this would make a fine marriage-home and all it needed was the emptying of a couple of drawers. She gave a fleeting thought to Brian's mother. With luck, she might drown herself in her incontinence within the year, and if not, then she would definitely have to be put away. She would have to broach the matter with Brian. There were so many things, she realized, she would have to ask him about, and she decided there and then to give herself a rehearsal. She would invite Maurice to dinner. But first she would clear out the spare room of all the old cases and cartons full of things that she couldn't bear to throw away. Now she would make a clean sweep of everything. She would give Brian space to leave his own individual traces; she would make him realize he could only gain by changing his status. As a preliminary she might even offer to do some of his small domestic chores like washing or darning his socks. But she would not give too much away, for fear he would take advantage. There had to be a threshold to her offerings. That would be constant and unmovable, until the time when a wedding-band allowed her to give her all. And she fell again to thinking of her wedding-day, and the time passed so quickly in her day-dreaming that it was soon close to supper-time. She decided to postpone the spare room cleaning and to make sure that Maurice had a good meal.

She set the table and hooked him gently on the wall. It was a long time since they had dined together and she felt guilty because of her neglect. She lit a candle and put it in the centre of the table. Maurice, too, was entitled to join in celebration. She adjusted herself opposite him and smiled. "I wish you a very Happy New Year," she said. He nodded, clearly wishing the same for her.

"Maurice," she began, "I want to discuss my future with you." She knew she must not ask him advice or indeed any question at all, because his lack of verbal response only served to shatter the illusion that she was not dining alone. "I'm a little bit worried about Brian," she went on. She thought that if she could talk about it, if she could let the fearful words out into the room, and air them a little, perhaps they would be satisfied and go away and not trouble her any more. "It's my investment," she said, airing every syllable. "It's over a thousand pounds now, and I don't know what he's done with it. He said he'd save it for me. You heard him yourself years ago. He said it was an investment, didn't he?" She looked at Maurice and saw that he remembered. "Well, he doesn't mention anything about it. And I'm afraid to ask. I'm afraid to ask him," she repeated and paused, hoping to get some answer from its echo. "I'm afraid he'll be angry if I ask him." Suddenly the need to verbalize the core of her anxieties nagged at her throat, and she got up for she didn't need Maurice as eavesdropper, and she whispered softly, for she herself didn't want to hear, "I don't think he's saved it at all. I think he's spent every penny." She felt a tear trickle down her cheek and she sat in her place again and noticed that Maurice was weeping, too. "I'll speak to him tomorrow," she practically shouted at her companion. "I'll have it out with him. Penny by penny. My diary will order it," she screamed. "Then I'll *have* to do it." Her anxiety eased a little with this decision, painful as she knew its consequence might be. Yet despite the relief, she was trembling pitifully, and she knew it as a sign of the hatred growing inside her, a hatred and mistrust for the man on whose behalf she had this day ordered her bridal gown. On whose behalf she had re-planned her own home, accommodating him with gentle consideration. But she didn't want to hate him. He had, after all, given her a great deal of pleasure. She looked up at Maurice. "What does it matter," she said, "even if I did pay for it? I've paid much more for things that I didn't enjoy at all." She wanted to tell him a story that would illustrate such pointless expenditure. But she could look back on little pleasure in her life, whether paid for or otherwise. "Well, it doesn't matter," she said. She was on the point of asking Maurice point-blank for his advice. She experienced a brief moment of total belief in the flesh of her companion. It did not last long, and for that she was grateful. She wondered why she was grateful. Maurice was patently there. Anybody could see him. She looked at him and she didn't understand him at all. "We must keep our wits about us, mustn't we, Maurice?" she said. "Tomorrow we'll tackle him." Mute as he was, she enlisted him for support, and to that end she decided to use him for a dummy run.

"Brian," she said, looking at the mirror, "what have you done with my savings?" Maurice turned up his nose. That approach was no good at all. It was much too direct and allowed for an outright negative answer, after which the subject was closed.

She tried again. "I read in the paper last week, Brian, that lots of people are putting their money into building societies." She looked at Maurice for an assessment of her more oblique approach. It had pleased him and he smiled. "We can always go on from there, can't we?" she said. "I'd let you stay in the room, Maurice, you know I would, but I think Brian might be a bit embarrassed. But I'll tell you about it afterwards. Every word, I promise." She smiled at him, hoping to disguise her feelings of treachery for she wanted him away, back on the floor and out of her face and mind. "I'm going to make an early night," she said to him. "We'll have dinner together again tomorrow." She got up from the table, and without looking at him, she lifted him gently off the wall. "I'll talk to him tomorrow," she said to no-one in particular, and had she been brave, she would have ordered it in her diary there and then. But she rationalized her reluctance by reminding herself that each day prescribed its own event and to precipitate an order would invalidate its purpose as a diary. When it was convenient, she thought of it in that way, but mostly she no longer understood what the little green book had become. The only thing she knew for certain was that she had become utterly dependent on it, and its benevolent tyranny frightened her.

12

"YOU WANT TO GET RID OF ME," MRS. WATTS SAID. IT WAS AS good a way to begin a new year as any.

"If you don't want to go," Brian said, confident in the suitcases at her feet, "nobody is forcing you. For years now you've been nagging to go to The Petunias. Now it's all settled, my job will see to that, and you can live in comfort for the rest of your life. But if you don't want to go," he said, making to take off his coat, "we can go on as before."

She wanted to go, desperately. All night she hadn't slept in her excitement, and in the morning the bed was sodden. Brian had tipped the mattress out of the window, and he resolved to burn it as soon as he got back home.

"What will you do without me?" she nagged. "How are you going to manage?"

"Don't worry about me," he said. "I'll manage alright." Then, as a small concession, which he could now afford as he envisaged the freedom of his future, "I'll miss you, though," he said. He manufactured a smile, and she did likewise, for at bottom neither had any reason for affection for the other. She wouldn't tell him to put his coat on, because that would have been an admission of her desire to leave. "I'll have to go, I suppose," she said, "now that you've paid out all that money."

But Brian wasn't giving an inch. He wasn't going to budge until she told him outright that she wanted to go. "Don't worry about that," he said, "it's only a deposit. I can get it back." Stalemate.

"But the others there are expecting me. Especially Miss Winters. She'll be disappointed if I don't come. I can't let her down."

"I think she'll get over her disappointment," Brian said, and he had the actual gall to sit down and open his jacket and slip off his shoes as if he had a mind to spend the day at home.

Mrs. Watts was crestfallen. "Oh, we'd better go," she said after a while.

"Why?"

"Because you've arranged it all," she screamed at him.

Brian shrugged. "So I can un-arrange it," he said.

She started to cry. Brian knew the tears were real. "D'you *want* to go or don't you?" he said mercilessly.

She nodded in submission and Brian put on his coat. "I'll go and find a taxi," he said. "You wait with the cases in the hall."

He walked down the street to the main road junction. A passer-by would have thought him a self-made man, full of confidence and knowing exactly where he was going in his life and to what purpose. And indeed the judgement would have been correct, for Brian envisaged his future with the utmost precision and content. Unlike Miss Hawkins, he had regularly taken stock. He had all the data he needed. His income fluctuated, but he had enough regular clients to more than cover his basic needs. And the most important of these was a reliable guarantee to petunia his mother.

He had done rather well in the past few years. He had as much business as he desired. More would have taxed his energies, and would thus diminish the quality of his services. His business had been built up almost entirely on recommendation. After his fortuitous meeting with Mrs. Makins, he no longer had any need to frequent libraries or supermarkets for clientele. Mrs. Makins had a friend and she, another, and Brian served along the grape-vine, and always left by the back-door. Over the past year a few clients had died on him, one actually in his arms in the middle of a £3 all-in cuddle. He'd straightened her out on the settee and adjusted her dress. Then he crept out of the back-door like an assassin. That experience had unnerved him considerably, and he'd had to lay off for a while, pleading a cold to his clients via the post. He noticed on his return to work how the appetite doth grow by what it feeds on, and his good ladies were practically climbing the walls on his return. As a consequence, he introduced occasional 'flu into his time-table, and his turn-over rose proportionately. Most of his ladies had gravitated to his specialities. And this category had increased considerably. Mrs. Makins had taught him a great deal, learned no doubt from her husband's "little quirks," as she fondly called them, though there was nothing little about them, and certainly they were not fond. Brian had also listed an appendix category, which he called supplementary benefits, and they were certainly beneficial. Most of his ladies had dispensed with the first and second categories, because if they were served with the rest, they discovered that the hors d'oeuvres were an inevitable accompaniment. The climax of Brian's services was almost anatomically impossible without a certain amount of his cheaper offerings. So over the years Brian Watts had made a tidy sum. With it, he'd bought new suits and an occasional box of chocolates for his mother. And he always took a bunch of flowers to Mrs. Makins, because she had done so much to enlarge his clientèle. He would never have believed that so many women felt the need of such services as his, and he could only conclude that by paying for it they could have it only when they wanted it, and the cash ensured their honesty and independence. He wondered whether Mrs. Makins felt that way. He was becoming quite attached to her. He respected her because she never took advantage of her favoured position. She would have been entitled to ask for a commission, or some form of rake-off, but she insisted on paying her way like everybody else. But he had given one service to Violet that was not, and never would be, on his list. And he'd given it gratuitously and with pleasure. He had kissed her. He realized afterwards how exclusively it coloured their dealings. A kiss between two people, he surmised, spelt a relationship, while with all the kissless others, there was only connexion.

With all his clients, Brian had been scrupulously honest. They knew that servicing was his profession and out of it he made a clean and decent living. Miss Hawkins was the exception and the thought of her was the only scruple he allowed himself. She was being grossly deceived, he knew. He had been careful never to wear any of his new suits on his Miss Hawkins' visits, but appeared always in the costume of their first meeting. When he was with her, he had to conceal his developed virtuosity, though her simple requests called little on his skill. Nevertheless, simple and cheap as her needs were, they were monotonously regular, and gently he had screwed her out of a thousand pounds. And it worried him. Not the immorality of it, but the sheer difficulty of talking himself out of the swindle. She rarely enquired about the investments he had promised to make for her, and when she did, it was timid and easily fobbed off with his vague assurances. But one day she would be less timid, and demand chapter and verse. He could, of course, drop her. One of the bonuses of his trade was that fraud was easy, since no-one would have the courage to tell the police, but he still retained a small affection for his first client, though he pitied her for her parsimonious and schoolgirl requests. But he could hardly tell her that her money was well invested in The Petunias, but that it was an investment that paid no interest or return. For he had used it as an entrance fee, a fee that was obligatory, and only served to secure a place. It was not returnable, but a certain portion of it was put aside for funeral expenses. In the beginning he had put Miss Hawkins' money by as he had promised, but when the demand came from the home, he had to avail himself of it, for it was the only ready and large sum he had to hand. His other clients were steady enough to foot the weekly bill, but poor Miss Hawkins would never see her savings again. It sometimes occurred to him to give her his services gratis, simply to square his own conscience, but he feared the extremes she might infer from free trading. Now Violet was altogether a different kettle of fish.

As he waited on the corner for a taxi, he checked on his business diary. As he feared, he was due to serve Miss Hawkins the following day. He prayed that she would not celebrate the new year by enquiring into her accounts.

An empty taxi cruised to the kerb and he took it back to the house. His mother waited on the porch, her calf soldered to the suit-case, her eyes aglow with excitement, and a small puddle at her feet. She looked like a small evacuee. Brian picked up the case and she tottered a little. He took her arm. Then his mother did the most extraordinary thing. She slipped her hand down the sleeve of his coat and took his hand in hers. Never in his life had he held her hand, and now it felt like a snake on his palm and he very much wanted to be sick. He grabbed her elbow and practically shoved her into the car. She did not look back at the house as she left. Though she had lived there for well on sixty years, she gave it not a backward glance. Mrs. Watts had no sense of history and even less sense of her own failure, so she allowed herself no nostalgia either. Within a few weeks, she would even have forgotten the colour of the wall-paper. They were due to clock in at The Petunias just before lunchtime. Brian had arranged everything. He had managed to get his mother a room in the annexe of the house, which was slightly cheaper than those in the main building. She did, however, have her own bathroom, and the only disadvantage was that she would have to cross the lawns to reach the dining-room. She would have company though. There were four other ladies in the annexe, one of whom, a Miss Winters, had taken a particular liking to his mother. He himself had not warmed to the lady and sensed, too, that she was disliked by the other ladies in the block, who shunned her. Hence her relief at Mrs. Watts's arrival.

The taxi drove up The Petunia's carriage-way and set them down at the annexe door. A nurse greeted them, and showed the way to Mrs. Watts's room. Brian put the case on the bed, and before he could open it, Miss Winters appeared in the doorway. She was a stern-looking woman, and though her voice was a smiling one, there was an uncanny lack of smile on her face. The wrinkles, now honoured by time, had probably been there from birth, notched initially by a lack of loving and grooved over the years in the resulting acrimony. He would be delighted to leave them to-gether.

As Brian took his mother's clothes out of the case, he noticed how Miss Winters was making her way towards the bed, eyeing each item of clothing as if gauging Mrs. Watts's estate. Out of his immoral earnings, he had bought his mother new sets of underwear and a couple of floral frocks. When packing, he had interlaced each item with coloured tissue paper that he used to trace his bills of fare. The case looked like a honeymooner's. Miss Winters looked on with approval.

They heard a bell from across the lawns. "That'll be lunch," Miss Winters said. "Tuesday it's liver." Her voice betrayed a cer-tain relish for the dish, yet her face retained its air of stern disgust.

The nurse appeared at the door and invited Brian to stay for lunch. It was a courtesy invitation and offered to all those accom-panying the new inmates on their first day. He had a client at four o'clock, so there was time enough to dally. He accepted her offer and the nurse hurried away to inform the dining-room.

"Would you like to see my room?" Miss Winters said. "It's just next door." Mrs. Watts was curious, and she tugged at Brian's sleeve. They followed Miss Winters into her retreat. The room was identical with his mother's but as Brian stepped inside he had the impression that Miss Winters did not live alone, and looking around, it was clear that the lady lived with Jesus who was all over the walls and on every available surface. From behind the bed He proclaimed that He was Love. On the bedside table, He bled in plastic gore from His crucifix. On the mantelpiece, He lay in His manger, flanked by papier-mâché hay and cows. On the television cabinet, as if to offset the questionable goings on beneath Him, He posed as teacher, His hand outstretched towards the viewing sinner. The central piece was a ceramic model of the Holy Mother, cov-ered in a polythene bag. She only took it off at Christmas, Miss Winters told them, but she would make an exception now in order to show that the figure was not just a pretty face. By a simple twist of the arm, the Lady let forth a musical box version of "Silent Night, Holy Night." Miss Winters waited for the song to end, then she replaced the polythene bag. The room was a corner of Disneyland, and Mrs. Watts thought it was very pretty. She looked round the room for the relief of a secular image. On the dressing table, there was a large photograph of many people. It looked like a school outing. A stern young woman stood at their centre, and the children flanked her in a startled paralysis of fear.

"Those were my little orphans," Miss Winters said with pride. "The Sacred Heart Orphanage. I was Matron there." Her voice was suddenly gruff, and Brian noticed a sudden smile on her face, and he marvelled at how the two measures managed to operate so separately. Mrs. Watts was impressed. The Jesus paraphernalia belonged to her calling, so it was understandable. "I had forty girls and boys in my care," she said, "and they all grew up into God-fearing Christians. I was there for thirty years." The smile fell off her face and into her voice again, as she said, "After lunch, I'll tell you all about them."

The dining room was like that of an hotel. There were separate tables, and to each one, a vase of dusted petunias, hardy plastic perennials. The three of them were ushered by a uniformed waitress to a corner table overlooking the lawns, which was to be his mother's permanent and shared site. There were linen table-napkins and an abundance of silver cutlery and the poshness of it all made Mrs. Watts giggle. Brian feared for the inevitable puddle at her feet. Somehow, back in their old and dirty house, it didn't matter; the cracked lino on their living room floor had acquired a natural expectation for her incontinence. But now, on this thickly carpeted floor, in the midst of all this continent decorum, he would have felt deeply ashamed, and as her escort, marginally responsible. He looked at the carpet beneath her feet. It was mercifully dry. He looked about the room. There were about forty guests in the dining-room and most of them were women. For a moment he considered it as a client hunting-ground, but he quickly dismissed the idea, for it would have been poaching on his own door-step, and in any case, they were all too old for any service beyond his first nursery category. In his first year of business, he might have been grateful for their small donations, but now, with his expansion, he need no longer entertain the small fry. And once again he gave a fearful thought to Miss Hawkins, and the brown Windsor soup dribbled on his chin. If she brought the subject up on the following day, he would lie. He would tell her her money was safely invested. He thought he might work a little harder in order eventually to repay her and so be shot of her for ever. But he had to admit that he was physically incapable of taking on any more clients unless they needed only the first section, and that was boring work, and by the time he had deducted cost of travel, it was barely profitable. A thousand pounds meant years of hand- and leg-touching, and by now he was too hardened a professional for that kind of trivia. He needed to get his mind off Miss Hawkins, and though he was totally disinterested in Miss Winters' past, he urged her to tell them as she had promised.

Miss Winters was very forthcoming. "They were the happiest days of my life," she said, her miserable face denying every syllable. Indeed, even Miss Winters occasionally confessed to herself, surrounded as she was by all the trappings of contrition, that as Matron she had never been more miserable, but her subsequent retirement had been even more desolate. So her Matron happiness was purely retrospective. "I must confess," she said, "I preferred the little girls. They were so helpful about the house." Had she been honest, as she was on occasion, lying stiffly between the sheets beside Him who had died for the likes of her, she would have admitted that she did not prefer the girls to the boys. She simply loathed them less. But over the intervening years she had talked herself into the image of the loving and kindly mother-substitute, and most of the time she believed in her illusion. "I was an orphan myself, you see, so I knew their problems. But they were luckier than I ever was. I was brought up in a workhouse. I'm not ashamed of it," she almost shouted, "because I worked hard and I made something of myself."

Brian thought she was quite loathsome and a fit companion for his mother. "Of course you did. Any one can see that," Mrs. Watts said, and as she was speaking, she was wondering about her return service and how she could justify herself to this stern daughter of duty. "I think you could say the same for me, couldn't you, Brian?" With her cold eyes she dared him to deny it, and he, fearing the puddle, hastily agreed. "I was brought up in an orphanage, too," she lied. Or did she lie? Brian wondered, and he suddenly realized that his mother had never talked to him about her childhood. Her invective was confined to the years of her marriage, and the burden that Brian had been on her. Somehow he couldn't imagine his mother as a child, orphaned or otherwise, and he listened eagerly to the recital of her real or imagined childhood. When she mentioned the alms-house, Brian was suspicious, sensing that she was playing one-upmanship with Miss Winters, vying with her for the monopoly of deprivation in their formative years. But she gave its address, somewhere in the North of England, and she reeled it off with honest confidence. She'd left school when she was fourteen, she said, and like all the other girls, had gone into service. A variety of jobs followed, but she never rose above the rank of scullery maid. Miss Winters turned up her nose, not so much at the status itself, but that it betrayed a singular lack of initiative and efficiency on Mrs. Watts's behalf. Mrs. Watts caught her grimace, and pleaded that it was not her fault, that there was too much competition and that the head housekeepers were always against her. Miss Winters stiffened, as she had stiffened so many times in her Matron days when faced with laziness and insubordination. Poor Mrs. Watts knew that she had made a bad start, and she hastened to move on to the recital of her disastrous marriage, a subject which Miss Winters found much more to her taste, and with her smiling voice and rigid face she offered her profound sympathy. "Then I had him," Mrs. Watts said without looking in Brian's direction, "and that more or less finished me off."

For someone who'd been finished off, she looked pretty hale and hearty, but his mother was still insisting on her hardships and deprivation until even Miss Winters sought to change the subject, and preferably back to herself.

"I always saw that my girls understood marriage, and all the business that goes with it," she said quickly. "Before they left the Orphanage. I never ceased to remind them of the dangers that lay outside, and I gave them lots of tips to avoid them." Brian wondered if those tips had been based on personal experience, but looking at Miss Winters, it was difficult to imagine that her knowledge was based on anything but prejudiced theory. She was not exactly a repulsive woman, but there was something actively repellent about her. It was nothing definable like bad odour or ugliness. Miss Winters was over-clean and passing fair for her age. But she gave off a sour air of untouchability and a hint of dire consequences for anyone who so much as tapped her armour. But Brian was not tempted. He was happy to leave them to each other in their own life-enhancing bitterness.

After lunch, he took his mother back to her room and Miss Winters followed. She had a deep sense of her own privacy, but it did not extend to others. She hovered at Mrs. Watts's door as Brian took his leave. "I'll come and visit you," he said, "one day next week."

"Only if you want to," she said.

He didn't, any more than she wanted to see him. She saw herself settled for life in this luxury, and she was glad of it and she wanted no reminders of her pre-Petunia days.

"I'll come next week," he said. He didn't quite know how to say good-bye. Miss Winters' alarming presence on the threshold required, as audience, a formal farewell. He wasn't going to kiss his mother, and certainly he would not touch her snake-like hand. So he went behind her and pecked at her dowager's hump, noticing it for the first time. He backed towards the door. His mother wasn't even looking at him. She was busy putting a coloured glass paperweight on the mantelpiece. He sidled past Miss Winters, forbearing to touch her, too, and he was out of the drive and hailing a cab before they noticed that he had gone.

When he reached home, he saw her visiting-card on the cracked lino. It would be the last one she would ever leave in this place, and this thought gave him heart as he took the mop and cleaned it away. Then he put the evil-smelling mop in the dustbin, together with her mattress. He spent the next hour cleaning the flat of all her remaining possessions. As he swept under the bed, he noticed that she had forgotten her slippers, and he was about to send them to the dust-bin, too, but he had an abrupt and acute feeling that he was burying her alive. And all of a sudden, he missed her. He sat on the springs of the bed and tried to accommodate the feelings that were so alien to him. He told himself that she was better off where she was. He patted himself on the back that he had made it possible. She would eat well and be cared for, and she already had one friend, which was one more than she'd ever had before. And hadn't he kept her all these years on his moral as well as immoral earnings? But with all these rationalizations, he still felt an uncommon ache in his heart. Had he investigated further, he would have realized that the ache had less to do with his mother than with poor Miss Hawkins, whose cheese-paring slippers looked exactly the same. But no matter the cause, he wept, and his tears were on behalf of all the inde-cencies he'd ever committed, and all the love to which he'd never been able to surrender. For the first time in his life, Brian Watts ac-knowledged that, after all, he was only human.

13

MISS HAWKINS ROSE FULL OF RESOLUTE DECISIONS. SHE HAD promised Maurice that she would talk to Brian and she dare not let Maurice down. As far as she was concerned, she was happy to let matters slide, and to trust that Brian had invested her money wisely. But Maurice was worried on her behalf and it was only right that she should set his mind at rest.

As she crossed through the hall into the kitchen, she saw a letter in the box. There was no account due, and she wondered who on earth could be writing to her. She had a presentiment of bad news, and she picked up the letter and did not look at it until she'd reached the support of the sitting-room settee. On the back of the envelope was printed the name of her bank, and her stomach rumbled with fear. She opened it quickly, seeing no point in delaying the bad news. The letter was from her bank manager. He had noted with some concern, she read, the dwindling deposit of her savings, and he would be glad if she would come to the bank at her earliest convenience to discuss the matter with him. He added a P.S. to the letter, wishing her a Happy New Year, but it was clearly an after-thought, and, as such, held out little hope for her future prosperity. A surge of Brian-hate welled inside her, but she controlled it, knowing that the letter came as no surprise. She knew that she had been drawing on her savings, but what worried her was the bank manager's concern, which strongly reflected her own, and confirmed that she did indeed have something to be anxious about. She tried to cheer herself up with a cup of tea, and to convince herself that Brian had surely invested her savings. She decided to dress and go straightway to the bank so that she would be armed to face Brian in the afternoon. Whatever the outcome at the bank, the confrontation was imperative, so she opened her diary and wrote, "Tackled Brian (about my investment)."

The bank manager was delighted that she had answered the summons so promptly, but she found his solicitousness very unnerving. She sat opposite him at his desk, as he mulled over the thin file which lay before him. "To tell you the truth, Miss Hawkins," he said, "I'm a little worried by the state of your account. Especially your savings account and its dwindling condition." He looked up at her for some explanation.

"I've had a lot of expenses recently," she said, playing for time.

"They seem to be very regular ones," he said, "and have been going on for some time." Then mercilessly he itemized her weekly withdrawals, opposing their extravagance with her ludicrous income. She had the impression that she was on trial, and this fed a growing belligerence. She couldn't see that her private spending was any business of the bank manager, and she said as much in the politest possible terms. "I'm concerned about you," he said. "And your future. If this regular expenditure continues, in a very short time, my dear lady, you will be penniless."

His statement was unanswerable and there was a silence.

"Could you tell me how you are spending this money?" he asked kindly. "D'you have some debt or obligation?" He paused. "All this is absolutely confidential," he said. "You need have no fear about that."

"No," she heard herself shouting, "I don't owe a penny to anybody. I pay my way," she said.

"Yes, but for how long?"

"I give my money to a friend. He invests it for me." She felt she owed something to the bank manager for his concern.

"Could you tell me what he's invested it in? Is it stocks or shares or . . . ?"

She noted the suspicion in his voice. "I'm not quite sure," she said. "I'm going to see him this afternoon. I'll ask him. He said it's a good investment and I'm not to worry."

He could see the worry on her face. "But where are the returns, Miss Hawkins?" he said gently.

"I'll ask him," she said.

"Would you let me know?"

She nodded with little faith that she would ever have anything to tell him. The interview was obviously over. She got up and went towards the door. As she reached it, he said, "Is he a particular friend, this gentleman?" She felt a hot flush on her face, and it was an involuntary answer.

"Keep in touch, Miss Hawkins," he pleaded. He was genuinely worried now. In his work as branch manager in different parts of the country, he had seen enough old ladies who had been conned into parting with their savings, and it was always a "particular" gentleman, one who knew his way about the stock market, and would earn an enviable return. The pattern was always the same. He would notice a dwindling account, and he would call for a meeting, such as the one he had just conducted. He would keep a weekly eye on the withdrawals until finally there was nothing left. He wouldn't have to ask for another meeting. The lady in question would present herself voluntarily and in acute distress. And then the whole sorry story would spill across his desk and it was always the same. They had invested a last bid for love, and as the shares fell, they had in desperation invested more. Then the bottom had fallen out of the market and they were penniless. Miss Hawkins had £500 left in her account. At her rate of spending, she would be back at his desk within three months. For no reason that he could think of, he phoned his wife.

Miss Hawkins laid the trolley for tea and put out the glasses and the bottle of port. She took herself a generous swig to still the rage inside her. When the door-bell rang, all the questions gathered like a hostile army on the tip of her tongue, and when she opened the door, they retreated in humble confusion. She noticed how shabby Brian's suit was, and realized that it was the same he had worn on their first meeting. Her savings had certainly not gone into his pocket. He was clearly as poor as she was, and she pitied him. "A Happy New Year," she said.

"And the same to you."

"I've a feeling this is going to be a good year," she said, without any feeling at all.

"You always say that," he said, knowing exactly what she hoped by it, and each year ignoring his cue. He sat on the settee while she went into the kitchen to make tea. He looked around the room and suddenly found its familiarity highly irritating. On the trolley, the inevitable sponge cake that lay on his stomach from one week to the next. The bottle of sickly sweet port that she seemed to need before each spending spree, and the bowl of soft sugar that was always encrusted with tea-droppings. He thought affectionately of the dry sherry and savories on Violet Makins' trolley. Poor old Miss Hawkins had no class at all. He winced at the neat pile of silver spelling out the paltry limits of her investment, and he wondered why he bothered. Then he noticed, underneath the port bottle, a five-pound note, a sign that Miss Hawkins was graduating to another category. The prospect of higher profits pleased him, and he wondered whether she would ever make the full grade. There were a number of varied services she could buy for five pounds, and all would serve to give her an appetite for further exploration. Who knows, Brian thought, in time she may well turn out to be his best customer. He got up and himself drew the curtains. Then he lit the candles that she'd placed on the table. He waited at her service.

Before leaving the kitchen, she made herself read the diary's order, so that it was on her tongue as she poured the tea. But it turned into an offer for a nice piece of sponge and a little port to wash it down with. Brian had a distinct feeling of words unspoken or substitute words for a subject that refused to surface. He shifted uneasily on the settee.

"I wanted to ask you something, Brian," she said.

Here it comes, he thought, and he postponed it with a request for

139

more sugar. Then as he stirred his tea, he considered it more expedient if he himself were to introduce the subject and fraudulently set her silly mind at rest. "Before I forget," he said, "I must tell you about your savings."

She almost dropped the cup from her hand in gratitude.

"I've put them into tin shares," he said. "A friend of mine who knows someone on the Stock Exchange recommended them. They're very steady and they've even increased a little in value." He had no idea what he was talking about.

She took the plunge. "Can I get my money back whenever I like?" she asked.

"Not immediately," he said, playing for time. "You see, they were the sort of shares that you had to invest in for a minimum of five years. That's why I got them cheaply," he said. "But after five years," he said confidentially, giving himself extra time, "they'll be yours with interest." He sensed that he was probably talking a lot of poppycock, but he could depend on her ignorance of stock market practices as being equal to his.

She sipped her tea, reasonably satisfied. She had obeyed the order at least, or rather, it had obeyed itself. But she wanted to ask the full name of the shares so that she could tell her bank manager. But she was afraid that Brian might suspect that she didn't believe him and that she was making enquiries like a policewoman.

"What did you want to ask me?" he said, now that he felt on safer ground.

She hesitated and her eye caught the five-pound note under the bottle. "I thought I'd ask for your services in the third category." She giggled and blushed and spilled her tea, then added, "now that I know that I can afford it."

When the tea was finished, she took a fortifying swig of port, then trade began. In view of his nagging conscience, he threw in a few services for free, but he worried about the poor lady's greedy appetite, knowing that her pocket would never stretch to her full satisfaction. "Who knows," she was saying dreamily, "if my ship comes home, I'll be able to pay for everything you offer." Just saying it was a form of gratification, and she was delighted with the idea that she had discovered all on her own a verbal source of ecstasy that was entirely free. She said it again and trembled all over. She would try saying it to herself when Brian wasn't there, or if that didn't work, then to Maurice, who would have to listen because he had no alternative. She had a sudden surge of pity for her bank manager who didn't understand life at all.

Brian collected the money and decided to go home and change and take Violet out to dinner. As he was pocketing the change, she said generously, "That's your New Year present. Don't use it for the tin. Put it towards the cost of a new suit."

He shuffled down the road, knowing she was watching him from the window. It irritated him that he felt such a heel.

Miss Hawkins ticked off her diary's order. She tried out her verbal discovery in the silence of her curtained sitting-room, and found to her dismay that it didn't work. Maurice would have to come to dinner. But before that, she had to buy her wedding-dress material. She was glad that she would draw another cheque to annoy the bank manager. She gave Brian time to leave the vicinity, then she put on her coat and left the house.

"Tin," she said to herself, and again, "tin," regretting its syllabic shortage which seemed to reflect a lack of worth and returns. Yet it was an essential commodity even if not a luxury one. As she walked along, she noted everything that required some form of tin in its making, and by the time she reached the shop, she concluded that the world would fall apart were it not for that monosyllabic piece of merchandise, and that Brian had made a very sensible investment indeed. "Tin," she said once again as she entered the shop, and already her shares had soared.

She was not going to skimp on the material, she decided. She was going to buy the very best. A heavy white satin, Mrs. Church had said, and a length of silk net. She would not have to explain that it was for her wedding. The choice of materials made that abundantly clear, and she looked forward to showing off to the salesgirl that she, Miss Jean Hawkins, was a wanted woman.

She went up the lift to materials. She was disappointed to find that all the assistants were male. What's more, they were all young and cocky-looking, and their self-confidence and youth unnerved her. She looked around and picked on the very youngest of them, who perhaps had not yet caught the arrogance of those who thought they'd inherited the world.

"Can I help you, madam?" he said.

"I'd like to see some heavy white satin," she said, "and some silk net."

He winked at her and disappeared, but he was back before she had decided whether or not he had insulted her. He laid the cloth on the counter. She fingered it.

"It's a wedding, isn't it?" he said, marvelling at his powers of deduction.

She felt herself blushing. "That's right," she said.

The assistant was a chatty lad, and new at the game. He was a nosey parker, too. "Your daughter getting married, is she?"

Again Miss Hawkins had to consider whether or not the lad was being offensive. On the one hand, he'd not entertained the possibility of herself as a bride, yet on the other, he'd happily envisaged her as a mother. Miss Hawkins decided that the balance was even.

"Is that the best you have?" she said.

"It's the only white satin. It's specially made for weddings," he said.

She was glad not to have a choice. "I'll have eleven yards," she said as Mrs. Church had ordered her. The silk net, too, was a straightforward purchase. She watched him as he measured the cloth. He gave her a little extra. "That's for luck," he said, and he winked again. He wrapped it carefully. "That'll be thirty-seven pounds," he said.

"Will you take a cheque?"

"Of course," he said.

She wrote it out, chuckling to herself with tin and bank-manager thoughts. The boy took it to his superior who was standing at an adjacent counter. He looked at the cheque and motioned to the boy that he would deal with it himself. Miss Hawkins trembled. The man was courteous.

"We're not allowed to take cheques over thirty pounds without checking first with your bank. So if you'll give me a moment, madam, I'll make a phone-call.''

She nodded, trying to hide her fear. When he had gone she looked about her, expecting immediate arrest. It crossed her mind to leave the shop there and then. There'd been no order in her diary to buy the material. The act, she thought, was so easily executed. It was too unprofessional for her little book. So she could leave the shop without any risk of disobedience. Yet Mrs. Church could not lift a finger without the material, and so in a roundabout way, she would be revoking an earlier order. She decided to stand her ground. She looked about her haughtily as if nothing were amiss or ever likely to be, while she imagined the conversation that was buzzing over the wires between the well-intentioned assistant and her speechless and spluttering manager. She fully expected that in his tin-ignorant rage, he would simply replace the receiver. And she worked herself into a state of indignation that anyone should question her solvency. But the counter-hand returned smiling.

"That was alright," he said, and he handed over the parcel. Now she had nothing to do with her gathered indignation, so she modulated it to dignity, and with her head held high, she left the shop.

On her way home, she called in on Mrs. Church. The dressmaker told her that she could fit her in sooner, since the wedding she had been preparing for had been cancelled. "They changed their minds," Mrs. Church said. "Well, better before than after." Miss Hawkins took it as an ill omen, and wondered whether she should change her dress-maker. But Mrs. Church was stroking the material with such affection that it would have been cruel to deny her, and an arrangement for fitting was made for the following week. Miss Hawkins looked once more at her cherry-blossom pattern and was delighted. She would tell Maurice about it at dinner.

As she passed the newspaper stand at the corner of the street, she saw a headline in the early evening paper. "Fulbright freed." The name was familiar and attached to a gruesome affair many years ago. She could not remember the exact story, so she bought a paper to jog her memory. When she reached home, she put Maurice on the wall, dusting him down gently with her handkerchief. There was no need for him to be alone until supper-time. He could watch her while she read.

After the first few sentences, she recalled the whole story. It had been a particular recollection of hers, because the crime had been perpetrated on the very day of her promotion to head cashier, and she'd felt ashamed to be so elated when Fulbright's poor victim had so cruelly met her death. There was a quarrel, Fulbright said in his confession, and he'd pushed his wife into a blazing log fire, held her down and watched her burn. He was sentenced to thirty years' imprisonment, and the hanging brigade had come out in force. She remembered that on her way home from the factory that day, she'd been forced to make a detour to avoid the crowd of eager volunteers to put a rope round Fulbright's neck. And now he was free. He'd been a model prisoner, the report said, and had earned full remission. She worked it out quickly. Fulbright had been inside for twenty years. It was logical that she should relate his experience to her own. When her sentence had been passed, and during the last few years, she had never considered remission as her legal right. She had been a model prisoner. Of that there was no doubt. She had obeyed every single order and the confetti of little red ticks in her green book was testimony to her excellent behaviour. She was entitled to remission, and it was a legal entitlement. She started on her calculations, and then refrained. The fear that she might already be free confounded her. What would she do with her freedom, with her orderless days? She could not afford to be free. At least, not until she had become re-fettered, and that meant marriage to Brian. That meant another source of order and command. Brian would replace the little green book, and she would continue to live in the daily fulfilment of duty. She could not resist the temptation to add up her months of detention. They totalled sixty, which, minus a third in remission, gave her forty months to serve. She was surely near the end. She dared herself to work it out. On her careful reckoning, try as she did to err on authority's side, she had two months more to serve. "It's enough," she said to Maurice. "It's got to be enough. My dress must be ready in time." She was more concerned with the availability of a bridal gown than with someone along whose side to wear it. She was not worried about Brian. She knew that it was only his shyness that prevented the offering of a free hand. Over the next few weeks, she would encourage him, and, if pushed for time, her diary would finally order the proposal. "Maurice," she said, "I'm inviting you to the wedding. You'll be our most important guest. We'll have the reception in this room, so that you'll feel at home."

She decided to make a guest-list. It was her job to organize the wedding. She would trouble Brian as little as possible. She sat with the blank piece of paper in front of her, chewing the end of her pencil. She couldn't think of a single name. The two salient locations of her life were the Orphanage and the factory, and out of neither could she dredge a single invitee. She would have had poor Morris for sure. She looked around for her knitting, but postponed her anger till she had at least made a start on a guest-list. She scratched in her mind for a name. There was a group of people in the cashier's office, and all those with whom she had worked daily for over forty years. They would be bodies good enough to fill her sitting-room, but she couldn't for the life of her remember a single name. Suddenly she recalled Mr. Connell, the shop steward. He would do. She would go back to the factory on a visit, she decided, about a week before the wedding, and she would identify the faces by name and issue a blanket invitation. Then there would be Brian's mother, and possibly he had one or two friends he would want to invite, though she doubted it, feeling his isolation as acute as her own. She would have to prepare the wedding breakfast, too. Perhaps Mrs. Church would help her, and she was suddenly excited at the prospect of a real live name with familiar face attached, as a guest and possible helper in the preparations. And if there was a Mr. Church he could come, too. The room was filled to overflowing. There would have been no room for poor Morris anyway, and her swaying shadow became a merciful blur. For the first time in many years Miss Hawkins hoped that Matron was still alive, and perhaps findable, so that she could give her to understand that her starched guardian blight had not, after all, utterly managed to destroy her. This thought was not quite enough to keep her from her knitting, but it needed only a few plaining lines to stitch her irritation away. She put down her needles and looked in the mirror. "Maurice," she said. "I've decided that you shall give me away." He was all things to her, husband, brother and now father, all that she had never known, a kindred of boot-blacked mercury.

14

A MONTH LATER, MISS HAWKINS COLLECTED HER WEDDING-
dress. That morning she'd had another letter from her bank. It
queried her lack of acknowledgement of an earlier letter inviting
her to discuss once again her financial entanglements. It wondered
whether she had been out of town. It suggested that at her current
rate of spending she would soon be into an overdraught situation
without any visible securities. Would she please call in and clarify
her position. The letter was angry in the politest terms, and she
chose to ignore it as she had done its forerunner.

If she pretended that the letter wasn't there, it would cease to
exist. After reading it, she had hidden it away, and so successfully
that she had already forgotten its hiding place. She made sure the
cheque-book was in her bag before leaving for Mrs. Church's, and
she was out of the house and half way up the street before she remembered that there was no current order in her diary. Lately, as
her sentence drew near to its close, her fear of the little green book
had become more and more acute, as if each dwindling prison day
made a greater demand on her obedience.

She went back to the house. When she opened the diary to the
current page, she found an order already inscribed. She shivered.
She had absolutely no recollection of writing it. Yet it was without

doubt in her own handwriting. She read it with fearful curiosity. "Sold some furniture," it said. She was horrified. In the light of the letter from the bank manager, it was the obvious thing to do. But the idea of selling up her home, even marginally, was a frightening one, unless, of course, she cheered herself, unless it were in the name of matrimony. She convinced herself that that must have been the point, conscious or otherwise, of the order, and she set to making a list of near-dispensables. She wrote out a little card, advertising items of furniture for sale, giving her name and address. On her way to Mrs. Church's, she took it into the news-agent's shop, and paid for a week's display. The discovery of the day's order weighed heavily upon her and desperately she tried to recall writing it down. Over and over again, she recollected every movement she had made since rising. Her ablutions, her dressing, her collection of the post and hiding of same, but where, she had forgotten. It was therefore possible, she realized, to have forgotten the writing, too, but such a devastating order was, to say the least, memorable. In all her activities that morning, she simply could not see herself standing over the diary, her pen in her hand. She envisaged herself doing just that, but it was totally unreal and simply did not belong to that day. She was profoundly disturbed by the incident, for she feared the irrevocable lengths to which it might lead. As if her impending freedom was threatening her own free will. She was frightened. The element of the unknown and uncontrollable that had, that morning, slipped into the back door of her life could colonize her for ever, with heaven knew what consequences. She would watch herself, she decided. She would watch her every move, but she knew it was her thoughts that needed watching. The writing was a mere formality, and how could one set a sentinel on the mind? She trembled. She was glad to reach Mrs. Church's house.

The dress was laid out in the bedroom, draped over the counterpane, the cherry-blossom tiara at its head. Miss Hawkins burst into tears, and Mrs. Church took it as a compliment. "It *is* beautiful, isn't it?" she said. "Try it on, dear."

But Miss Hawkins was not weeping for its beauty. She wept for the hollowness of it, for its utter lack of habitation. Try as she would, she could not envisage herself inside, and as she stood there, willing herself into its satin folds, it took on the gentleness of a winding-sheet, and in such a manner, it shrouded her.

"I haven't time to try it on," she managed to say.

"Then I shan't ever see it." Mrs. Church was disappointed.

"I'll ask you to the wedding," Miss Hawkins said, clinging with a frantic despair to the frayed remnants of her fantasy.

"And when is that going to be?"

"Next month," she said. "I'll send you an invitation." She took out her cheque-book and wrote out the required amount, omitting to fill in the stub since there seemed to her no longer any point in itemizing money that simply wasn't there.

Mrs. Church wrapped the dress tenderly and with disappointment. She was surprised at how well it had turned out and it had given her confidence to scout for other orders. She was the second person whom Miss Hawkins had unknowingly launched into business.

When she got home, she checked on her diary. The order was still there, and simply required ticking off. But there was less joy than usual in the credit, for she was simply not wholly convinced that the order had been hers in the first place. She unwrapped the dress and was sorely tempted to try it on. Perhaps seeing herself inside it would revive the dying embers of what she knew now to be an illusion. She opened her mouth involuntarily, and as the words came out, she heard herself calling to Maurice. "Would you like to see my dress?" She was suddenly glad that the reality of Maurice had persisted, and if he was there, waiting for the bridal parade, then so would Brian wait at the altar, and Mrs. Church at her attending side, and the bank manager, tin-satisfied in the aisle.

She ran into the bedroom. She kept her eyes shut as she put the dress on, feeling for the small pearl buttons that ran from neck to waist. She opened her eyes only to put the tiara in place, and even then she avoided the full-length mirror, and concentrated only on a small hand-mirror, large enough to contain the reflection of her head. When the tiara was fitted, she held the mirror at arm's length. Her sheer delight in the results swept away once and for all the doubts that had accumulated in her mind. She was a bride-to-be, and the train proclaimed that certainty.

She turned to face the full-length mirror. Her reflection astounded her. Mrs. Church's doubts as to the fitness of the childish style would have been steadily confirmed had she seen her model on display. But Miss Hawkins saw only that which her wishful thinking prompted, and with this blinkered view, she saw a picture of youth that was nothing faded by delay. Through the virgin veil, she saw a bright hope for the future, a logical entitlement of the very young. She forgave the years that had stumbled by, stunned by non-events, and the disappointments and griefs of her childhood years. All but one.

Miss Hawkins shut her eyes tightly, trying to obliterate the naked bathroom bulb, caressing with its tender shadow the twisted rope of unwanted womenhood. Not to be forgiven. Never. "I hope Matron's dead," she hissed. "I hope she's in hell. I hope every part of her is burning slowly. Slowly enough to last for ever. Kill, kill." She felt the words hiss out of her mouth like a snake. They were words to eat, to relish, to regurgitate and relish again. "Kill, kill," she shouted, and she opened her eyes and wondered what devil had crept inside her, and wondered whether it had been there all along, and writing orders in her diary when she wasn't looking. She laughed aloud because she had to, else she might have given a small credence to the untenable thought that had crossed her mind. "I'm a bride," she said to the mirror, "and in a few weeks, I shall be Mrs. Brian Watts. I'm coming Maurice," she called, and she swept her train into the sitting-room.

She sat opposite him at the table. "D'you like it?" she said. He smiled. "But you can't see it all. I'll stand on a chair." She aligned a chair in front of the mirror, and presented Maurice with the whole of her. She hoped he had some sense of perspective. His moustache was aligned with her waist-band, and she had the impression it drooped a little. "Now don't sulk, Maurice," she said, "we're still going to be friends. You'll come to dinner like always, but Brian will be here, too." Once again, the slippery dream had found a secure foothold. She poured herself a little port and drank to her future.

The door-bell rang. She was expecting nobody. It had to be Brian, she thought. He was coming without an appointment. He was coming for free, to offer to donate his services to her for ever. It was no accident that she was trying on her bridal gown. It was because she knew, deep in her heart, that today he would come to claim her. She rushed into her bedroom to remove the evidence of her brash anticipation. It took her some time to undo the buttons, as the door-bell rang again and again. "I'm coming," she shouted. She laid the dress on the bed and covered it with a blanket. Brian must see no evidence of her expectation. She assumed a look of surprise on her face and opened the door.

"I believe you have some furniture for sale," the man said.

The first of the bailiffs had arrived.

Brian was stock-taking. He looked up from his ledger and sniffed at the dinginess that surrounded him. His mother's presence had somehow validated the dreariness of the flat. Her absence now only served to accentuate it. He had to get out of there. But he didn't have enough money to buy a new house. There was only one solution. Could he afford to give his services to Mrs. Makins for nothing? Could she, as his wife, live comfortably and acceptingly on his immoral earnings? He totted up his weekly income, excluding his favourite customer. It was more than adequate. Violet would certainly not want him to retire. What he liked most about her was that she recognized his trade as legitimate. She acknowledged the need for such a service, and often wondered why it was not officially licensed. He had no doubt that Violet would accept him. Often enough she had hinted at a need for a constant companion, but he did not intend to take up her suggestion until his income had stabilized. Besides, there was the question of poor Miss Hawkins, in whose simple mind dwelt the hopes and aspirations of the new Mrs. Watts. And expectations that he himself had shamefully nurtured. For the first few years of their trading, he had been unspecific about her savings, and his vagueness had led to conjecture on her part with a strong bias towards matrimony. Even when he translated her savings into fictitious tin, the goal of her expectations remained stable. She had hinted at it often enough. Any day now, he dreaded she might propose to him, or insist on getting her money back, or at least some concrete evidence as to its returns. He could, of course, drop her entirely, but such a course of action entailed a risk. She might pursue him with tears and demands, and he could accommodate neither. He would have to sit it out and pray for some small miracle. Meanwhile his lies and oblique promises would delay for ever the final show-down.

He wanted to get Miss Hawkins off his mind so that he could concentrate on Violet and the bonuses he could reap from a lifelong partnership. He liked her sitting-room very much. It was the first advantage that occurred to him. He saw himself lounging on her velvet settee, sipping sherry, and with no obligation to exert himself in any capacity. In time, the uniformed George would quietly and decently quit his silver frame to make room for his replacement. The conservatory that adjoined the sitting-room, he would turn into a studio, and get back to painting again. Bugger Miss Hawkins. He would propose to Violet this very day.

He put on his best suit, the pin-stripe that was her favourite, and set out to offer her his gratis hand. On the way to her house, he bought a large bunch of red roses, and holding it before him like a shield, he rang her bell. She was surprised to see him, but there was no question of her delight. He had caught her off guard. Her hair was loose and she was without make-up. He was rather surprised at the change in her and he donated a split-second to a second thought. But the lure of the cosy sitting-room won the day.

"I wasn't expecting you, Felix," she said.

Over the years, he had become used to his alias. He was known to all his clients as "Felix," all but Miss Hawkins, who simpered "Brian" at every turn. His name was the only truth he had given her. He would stick to "Felix," he decided. It had a ring of sophistication far more in tune with his present mode of living than the pedestrian "Brian." Yet sooner or later, and on some pretext, he would have to unveil "Watts," for it concerned Violet, and he wanted his marriage document at least to be legally above-board.

He pushed the flowers forward as she urged him inside. "It's not my birthday," she said.

"But it's a special day anyway. I've got something to say to you." The red roses and the pin-striped suit already shrieked what he had in mind, and though she had expected it for many months, it now took her by surprise. She wished she were properly dressed. "Have a sherry," she said, pouring him one. "And give me a few minutes. I want to change."

He was glad she had left the room, for that gave him an opportunity to view in detail his new estate. He took an overall sight of it, and decided that little needed changing. The conservatory, though, would need a thorough overhaul. At the moment it was full of crates and suitcases. She would have to store those somewhere else. He looked at the sideboard and noticed a gap in the picture gallery. George, silver frame and all, had disappeared. Was Violet expecting his proposal, or had George simply melted away in the natural passage of time? He hoped Violet had held on to the frame. He rather fancied himself in a silver lining. He heard her coming down the stairs and he sipped at his sherry.

She was wearing a dress he had never seen before. It was tightly fitting and outlined a surprisingly youthful figure. Usually on his visits, she wore a loose fitting house-gown, her "service wear," he called it, a comfortable garment that oiled the wheels of his trade. This present apparel seemed to declare a lack of service need, and would he state whatever other business he had in mind. He was glad that she was smiling, else he might have been wary of his proposal. She sat next to him on the settee, but at a distance. "Now what is it you have to say?" she said.

"I've come to offer you a lifetime of free service," he said.

She raised her eyebrows questioningly. She thought she might have understood him, but she was not quite sure. "Why me?" she said. "And can you afford it?"

"I've other clients as you know," he said, slightly put out by her lack of enthusiasm. "We'd have enough to live on."

Then she understood fully. "We?" she said.

"I'm asking you to marry me."

She took his hand and laid it on her forbidding skirt. "Oh, Felix," she said, "I can't say I wasn't expecting it. I've been hoping for it for a long time."

"Then you will?" he said.

"I'd be honoured to change my name to Hawkins."

He began to sweat a little.

"Is there anything the matter?" she said. "You're suddenly very pale."

"It's about Hawkins," he said. "There isn't any tin."

"Pardon?"

Then he realized he was pleading guilty in the wrong court. "Oh, nothing," he said, "it's just a line of a song I remembered." He was rather pleased with his quick cover-up, and it gave him confidence to bury his alias handle, and to offer her the poor but honest substitute of Watts. She understood the necessity for his pseudonym, but she was glad he'd been straight with Felix, she told him. It was such an exotic name. And he didn't have the heart to disabuse her.

"Mrs. Violet Watts," she tried.

"Will that suit?" he said.

She smiled. "I'll get used to it, I suppose. There's one thing though. About our marriage, I mean."

"Anything you ask for, dear."

"I want to go on paying," she said.

"But why? I shall be your husband. You'll have your conjugal rights."

"I want to pay," she said stubbornly. "Don't you see, that's half the fun."

No, he didn't see, but he was not displeased. His marriage would mean no drop in income. Violet was a woman in a million. "If that's how you want it," he said. "But I think it should go into a joint account."

"No," she said, "it will all be for you. Don't you see, dear," she said patiently, "I *need* to pay."

She's crackers, he thought, but as a profitable lunacy he was more than prepared to accept it.

They decided on an Easter wedding. At least, that was Violet's decision. She said it would be advantageous as far as tax was concerned. He explained that his was hardly a declarable income, and that since he never paid any tax, he didn't see how he personally could reap any advantage from her timing. And then Violet put her fiscal cards on the table. She had a tidy little income of her own. The terraced house next door belonged to her as well as the one on the other side, and lettings from both, together with her army pension, gave her a handsome income.

"I had no idea," Brian said, wishing to make it clear that he had not proposed for her money. Though it certainly was a happy bonus, he thought, and might even allow him to retire completely. Again he thought of Miss Hawkins and the tempting idea of dropping her entirely. The prospect of never having to enter that dingy sitting-room, never again to have to sip that sickly port, was distinctly appealing. He wondered what she would do if he never showed up again. She would go to his house, of course, and seek him out. He couldn't drop her until after he was married. Then he would move and leave no forwarding address. And she could never find him. For a few weeks she would go to the library and hang around the fiction shelves. She would go to her angry lonely bed each night and dream of tin, and the thought would cross her mind on waking that she must go to the police. Brian shivered at that possibility. All she knew about him was his name, old address, and description. It would be enough to start an investigation. But she dare not do it, he thought. She would have to tell the authorities all about the nature of their exchange, and poor and prim Miss Hawkins would shrink from such a terrible confession. He could rely on her fear and her prudery. He worked out the number of weeks until Easter. About twelve, he reckoned. Twelve more miserable Hawkins visits. But sixty pounds' worth of service. It would go towards the honeymoon.

"I would like to stay in this house," Violet was saying, as if Brian would voice an objection. "It would be silly to buy another house at today's prices."

"But I must pay the running expenses," Brian said. "I insist on that."

"Of course," she said, "otherwise you might feel like a lodger. Would you like to see the house?" she said. "After all these years, all you know is this room. And the bathroom. Shall we have a tour?" She gave him her arm and led him up the hall stairs to her bedroom. On his first visit to the house, he had peeked into the room, but he couldn't remember its dimensions or furnishings. It was smaller than he imagined, and the double bed took up most of its space.

"It's a single room, really," she said, as if by way of apology. "But I've always found it very cosy."

He would sleep on the right side of the bed, he thought, since that's how he always slept at home. Close to the door, and a means of escape. Besides, the lamp was on that side, and he liked to read in bed sometimes. And while he was dwelling on such nuptial thoughts, Violet interrupted him. "I'll show you your room," she said shyly.

She led him out onto the landing into an even smaller room. In it was a single bed, a tallboy and a small desk. "George used to like to have his private quarters," she said.

He was surprised that they were to be separated, but it rather pleased him. When occasionally he had fallen asleep in his own living-room, as a defence against his mother's constant harangue, she would often prod him into waking because his snoring got on her nerves. The distance between their two rooms, Brian gauged, was large enough to muffle his nocturnal music. Perhaps Violet, too, had a similar problem and had arranged for a carpeted no man's land to separate their private symphonies.

"It's very comfortable," he said.

She opened a drawer in the tallboy and took out two keys. "This is yours," she said, giving him one of them, "and this one is mine. I shall use it whenever I need your services."

"I'm a very lucky man," he said, and he meant it sincerely, but on his own account, without any complimentary reference to his future wife. And she, misunderstanding, was flattered, and declared herself likewise for having had the good fortune to meet him in the first place. "You know, Felix," she said, "you don't have to go on working. There'll be enough for both of us."

"A man has his pride, Violet," he said.

"Of course. But you could work part-time, and do a bit more painting."

It was an appropriate time to discuss the conversion of the conservatory.

"But where would I paint?" he said.

"In here. There's room for an easel and it's a very bright room. It faces south, and has the sun all day."

"I need a north light," he said, with the chill conservatory in mind. "Something on the other side of the house. Why not the conservatory? That would be ideal."

He saw her stiffen. The suggestion had plainly not pleased her.

"No, I'm afraid not," and there was a distinct distance in her voice. "Not the conservatory. That was George's favourite room. He used to sit there often, reading or playing patience. All his bits and pieces are there."

"Then I wouldn't dream of it," Brian said, knowing his place, but making a mental note to discover the meaning of her dear departed which she'd so graphically spelt out in his bits and pieces.

They were downstairs again. Brian felt that he had to make a solid contribution to their future partnership, and he asked her where she would like to go for the honeymoon. He had enough spare money for a week's extravagant fling, and if she was going to pay her service-way, it might stretch to a fortnight.

"Somewhere warm," she said. "I love the sun."

Warm at Easter was more costly. He hadn't reckoned on air-fares.

"We could go to Morocco," she was saying. "I've got a cousin who runs package holidays there. He might give us a free flight as a wedding present."

The woman had everything, Brian thought. He could hardly believe his good luck, and as a check of his good fortune, he felt bound to give a thought to the irritating Miss Hawkins. At such times, he really hated her. He had, after all, given her good value for her money. She couldn't expect that *and* an investment, too. There was no way he could pay it back. Except perhaps by telling her the truth, and offering her his services free until the debt was paid. But at the prudish rate she was spending, it would take him years to wipe the slate clean. And even if she were to buy such a proposition, he had little appetite for it. His heart would not be in his work, and as a result, his service would be slovenly. Not that poor Miss Hawkins would recognize a lack of skill, since she had no scale of comparison. He pitied her, and the more he pitied her the more he was irritated. No, he decided, he would drop her totally as soon as he was married.

"Morocco would be wonderful," he said. And as he looked at her in her tight-fitting dress, her eager face full of promise for the future, he had an overwhelming urge to make love to her. "Could I be of service to you?" he said, taking her hand.

"I don't need anything at present," she said.

"But I do," and he throbbed with a yearning he had never felt before. She looked him squarely in the face. "Then the tables are turned," she said with a smile. "And when that happens, *you* are the customer." He was delighted. It was a logical extension of their trading. "Are your prices competitive?" he said.

"They're the same as yours," she laughed.

Thus Mrs. Violet Makins, soon to be Mrs. Watts, made her first deal, and as a result of this turn of events, Brian saw his income reduced by at least half, and he resolved henceforward to curb his appetite, or he would end in bankruptcy.

But when Violet set about to serve him, Brian suddenly understood the power of paying for one's pleasure, and he, unobliged to raise a single finger, experienced for the first time the joys that lay on the other side of the counter.

When the deal was completed, he said, "I suppose I'd better have a key to your room too."

She smiled. "I'll give it to you on our wedding night," she said.

And so their marital future was put on a firm financial footing, and its eventfulness or otherwise depended on the generosity or meanness of spirit of each partner. Both of them were aware of the dangers of such a contract, and the possibility that thrift might drive them into mutual abstinence.

"One day a week, on a Sunday," Violet suggested, "we shall

both give our services free to the other.'' It was a clever move. The appetite must be fed, she knew, else it would atrophy completely.

Brian agreed readily, though he did not understand her motives. He could be sure of at least one day that, though unprofitable, would cost him nothing.

"Would you like to leave the wedding arrangements to me?'' she said.

He was glad to. She had, after all, been through it once before. "Just let me pay all the bills,'' he said.

"I think Easter Monday's a good day.''

He nodded, though Monday rang a distinctly irritating bell. It was Hawkins day, and it would mark the first Monday in many years that he would not spend with her. Yet he would serve her diligently and every week until that time, with promises for their united future, and tin-avoidance. And he would arrange to see her on the Easter Monday, too, and as she was sipping her courage port, her neat piles of silver coin on the table, the curtains drawn and the candles flickering, shivering for his ring on the front door, he would be well on his way to Casablanca, or wherever Violet's cousin had in mind, and he would be rid of her, leaden sponge and her uncut moquette for ever.

He rose to take his leave. "I'll see you tomorrow as usual,'' he said. "If you'll be needing me.''

"I'm sure I'll find the odd little thing for you to do,'' she teased.

He kissed her good-bye. A free special.

When he got home, he took out his ledger and looked up the Hawkins' account. He totted up her three-year expenditure. It came to £1255. Reckoning on £5 until his wedding day, he would be in her debt for over £1300. And though he had no means and even less intention of repaying her, he derived some satisfaction from knowing the exact sum of money the poor woman would never see again. It amounted to about half of the sums he had received from other clients in less than half the time. Serves her right, he thought, for being so cheese-paring.

15

OVER THE NEXT FEW WEEKS, MISS HAWKINS' FLAT TOOK ON A distinctly unfurnished look, as if it were untenanted, and every time she returned home, she wondered where it would all end. She consoled herself with the thought that her sentence was nearing its close and the automatic handmaid of her freedom was marriage. Then, in time, the accumulated interest on her tin would replace the furniture, and Brian would look after her for the rest of her life. There was no doubt in her mind that only shyness delayed his proposal. Perhaps she should encourage him more. She had bought a fresh bottle of port, a different brand this time, a vintage one, the shop-assistant had assured her, and much more potent. Perhaps it would bring her luck. She was due for servicing that afternoon. The shop-assistant's promise would be put to the test.

She had already sold her trolley, so she had to set out the service paraphernalia on the dining-table. Maurice looked down on the sponge and the bottle of port with faint disapproval, so she removed him from the wall. It was enough that she should judge herself, without any eyewitness accusation. She took him into the bedroom without looking at him, for she was suddenly ashamed. And in her shame, she became angry. She looked around for her knitting. It was not in its usual place, trailing its serpentine spleen from the small fireside chair that lay always within reach of her fury. And without looking anywhere else, she was acutely aware of panic, of a sense of terrible loss and desertion. She stood rigid in the middle of the room. She had a distinct impression of another presence in the flat, a manipulator, someone who wrote orders in her diary, someone who was selling off her furniture and now, as a last straw, had spirited away her anger-machine. "Hullo," she called out, and the echo resounded from the void where a sideboard once stood, and a cupboard, and a bookcase and all the bankrupt spaces of the room. She needed desperately to find the scarf, but at the same time she was terrified of looking for it. She knew it wasn't lost, but she feared the state in which it would be found, for she was sure it had unravelled its unending fury out of a sense of its own futility. For a moment she dared to allow herself to envisage a Brian-less future, and the thought of the penniless, possessionless years that it entailed was shattering. She rushed to her diary and opened it on the current page. "Proposed to Brian," she wrote, not wholly aware of the matter of her words, but knowing it as the only solution to all her problems. She returned to the sitting-room and sat down stiffly, her legs firmly crossed and trying not to think of the scarf, trying not to notice the unfamiliar and aching gaps around her, and not daring to think of what the diary had ordered. For all were stratagems of which she had no part, the machinations of a power outside herself, the promptings of the stealthy shadow of her own despair.

When the door-bell rang, she almost feared to answer it. If she refused to admit Brian, then she couldn't propose to him, and that would be a disobedience of the diary's order. For how could she propose to someone who just wasn't there? The bell rang again, rather faintly and without appetite, and she feared that if she didn't answer right away, he would leave, and possibly she would never see him again. At this thought, she bounded to her slippered feet and arrived at the front door breathless. Brian took her panting for lust, and a possible sign that after so many years she had decided to take the final plunge. She led him into the sitting-room.

If Brian noticed the denuded furnishings, he did not show it. His eye went straight to the piles of silver coin, and by their height, he gauged them as normal. In a way he was relieved. In view of his long term plans for poor Miss Hawkins, he was glad not to be offered her most valued possession, which year by year gathered worth like an antique. The leaden sponge sank on its plate on the table, and just looking at it gave him indigestion. He noticed that the label on the bottle was different. So, in a way, was Miss Hawkins' demeanour. The timidity was absent, and she looked almost angry. He began to fear that this meeting would be a turning-point in their affairs and that she would pin him down, once and for all, on his fraudulent tin, wanting to know its name on the market, its present price and the exact profits accrued over the years. He wanted very much to go away, but it was now too late to withdraw. "I haven't much time to-day, I'm afraid," he said. "My mother's not very well. In fact," he said, "would you mind if I came tomorrow? It would be much more convenient."

"Yes, I do mind," she said. "I'm busy tomorrow. All day." She couldn't postpone her diary's order. And she kept worrying about the scarf and the gaps in the room. And she began to dislike Brian, too, and with all these feelings of anxiety and displeasure, it was difficult to produce the accents that should accompany a proposal of marriage. She helped herself to some port and went into the kitchen to make the tea.

The diary lay open in front of the tea-caddy, though she could have sworn she had closed it, as she always did, for part of the pleasure of ticking was to open the book and find the right page, all teasing acts to postpone the thrill of climax. She saw the current order and knew that she had no alternative but to carry it out. She closed the book and locked it, then she manufactured a smile and carried in the tea.

He had drawn the curtains and lit the candles. She thought she would wait for the service to begin before plighting her troth on his shy behalf, since the words might then seem a natural result of his paid affections. She passed him his tea and cake, and sensing her unease, he decided to cheer her up. "I think we're due for another anniversary, my dear, you and I. Shall we drink to that?" He raised his cup and smiled at her, and she thought that he surely was on the brink of proposal. She waited, the cup to her lips, smiling. "To my first and only customer," he said.

She sipped some tea and waited again. He patted the settee beside him. She sat down, crossing her ankles and hovering on his next utterance.

"And what service does my ladyship want to-day?" he said. He put a gratis hand on her knee. The thought crossed Miss Hawkins' mind that for the first time she would actively disobey an order. It ran too much of a risk of his refusal, and he might never come again. And these were not pleasures she could easily forgo. Yet on the other hand there was no talk of her investment, and there was little enough left for her to live on. She took a deep breath and removed his hand. "Brian," she said.

He gulped his tea, and the resultant coughing fit postponed the show-down that he feared. He couldn't go on coughing for ever, but at least he'd stalled her prepared moment. "Give me a minute," he spluttered. She took away his cup, grinding her teeth, doubting that she could find the courage for a second attempt. She waited for the coughing to subside, then she handed him a little port. "That'll soothe your throat," she said. "Sip it gently."

He took it gratefully. Sickly as it was, it would prolong the delay, and give him time to think of a reason why she shouldn't be told the name of her shares. She hadn't given him much port, he noticed. Even with the tiniest sips it soon had to come to an end. Besides, she was standing over him, waiting for him to drain the glass. Then she sat down again with a determined look on her face that indicated that she was not in the least bit thrown by the coughing interruption. He trembled.

"Brian," she said again.

"What is it, my dear?"

"I think it's silly for us to go on like this."

For a moment there was a glimmer of hope. Was she, of her own accord, giving him the push? But then he realized that if that were the case, she would want to finalize her account. "Why not?" he said. "Don't you enjoy it?"

"Oh, yes, I enjoy it very much."

"Well, what is it then? Why can't we go on as before?"

"I would like something on a more permanent basis," she said. Now it was out, or almost all of it, enough to merit at least half a tick in the diary.

"But we are permanent," he said. "I've been coming here every Monday for over three years."

It was clear to her that he'd not got the message and again she feared his refusal. "I don't mean that," she said.

"Then what do you mean?" He regretted his question the moment it was out. He knew very well what she meant and he had given her carte blanche for a proposal.

And she took it readily. "Brian," she said.

He thought it was such a silly name, and the way she said it made it sound even sillier. She whined it like a cry of pain.

"I'm proposing to you," she said.

"Proposing what?" It was his last pathetic stand for delay.

"Marriage."

The word echoed round the empty spaces of the room, finding no obstacle that might have muted its doomed reverberation. Marriage. It was an offer of nothing but her impoverished availability. She unlocked her ankles, satisfied that she had done her duty. The tick was secure, which was more than she could at present say of her future. She hovered for his reply.

Again he temporized, taking her hand, his mind an utter blank.

"Well, what d'you think?" she said, encouraged by the hand-holding.

"Don't think I haven't thought of it," he said, "many times." Now having spilt the first falsehood, it was easy to elaborate, and he set off on a whirl of lies and fabrication, with a certain secret enjoyment, though he was careful to maintain a look of worried helplessness. "I just don't know how I can manage it," he said. "It's my poor mother." He tried not to think of her lapped in Petunia luxury, and probably at this very moment relishing the hot buttered scones of a Petunia tea. "I couldn't leave her," he said.

"You could put her in a home."

164

He smiled. "I couldn't afford that," he said.

"But there are homes on the National Health," she protested.

"No," he said, with determination, "I couldn't bring myself to put her in one of those." He saw her lip curl in anger, and he regretted the finality of his declaration, fearing that she would jettison all her marital hopes and in their stead make a desperate move to get her money back. "But don't give up hope," he said quickly. "I'll work something out. I promise I will."

She didn't quite see what he had in mind, but she was afraid to ask for details in case it would seem like nagging. "Are you sure it's only your mother?" she dared to ask.

She had given him a clue for another objection, and he was quick to grasp it.

"Well," he said, "it's a bit difficult to put into words."

"Go on," she said, encouraging. She was prepared to be anything for him, do anything for him, to remove whatever obstacle he had in mind. He for his part had hit upon the very stumbling-block that he confidentially knew Miss Hawkins would never surmount. "I know we've known each other for a long time," he said, "but well—well, we don't know each other all that well." He couldn't say "intimately." It was too brash and allowed for no misinterpretation. He preferred to leave it ambiguously in the air, so that she could do what she wished with it. And though Miss Hawkins knew perfectly well what he meant, she pretended it was beyond her understanding, so beyond in fact, that there was no point in elucidating. She quickly changed the subject. "Will you have another cup of tea?" she said, and as she poured she understood exactly what she had to do to win Brian's hand. She was delighted that the solution was so abundantly clear, yet the thought of its execution was devastating. But not to-day. The diary had not ordered it, and in any case she didn't have that kind of money, and no means of getting it, she thought, as she looked round the room, evaluating what was left of her chattels. If her eye rested on the settee, she told herself she was looking at Brian. That's all she was doing, she said to herself, simply because he was sitting there. "I've got five pounds to spend," she said, like a child in a toyshop. It was what a dealer had given her for a gold Armistice medal that was found around her neck when the wrapped-up bundle of her was delivered to the Sacred Heart Orphanage. It was sufficient evidence to prove to Matron that the infant had been sired by a common soldier with the help of an even commoner camp-follower, and the medallion was never removed so that it should serve as a reminder of the nothingness from which she came. Miss Hawkins had worn it most of her life, thinking it was probably a birth mark. Until one day at the factory when the fudge-wrapper foreman saw it as an opportunity for mamillary investigation and whipped it out of her cleavage. His interest in the medal soon superseded that of its nestling-place, and he turned it over and over with envy. "Worth quite a bit, that is," he said. That day Miss Hawkins took it off her neck as much for its value as to discourage further lecherous probings. She kept it in a little box on her dressing-table, her only clue to her parentage. Now she had sold it for her pleasure. According to Matron's standards, her parents would have been proud of her.

She drew the curtains, lit the candles, but this time she had to admit that there was less pleasure in their exchange. She was anxious to get it over with, to spend her money quickly, so that he would go away and leave her alone to tick off the little order in the book. More and more she realized that this act was the major pleasure of her life as well as its prime justification. She didn't particularly want to marry Brian. She was wedded to her diary, a union as tyrannous as it was pleasurable. But the diary couldn't support her. It couldn't replace her furniture or underwrite her weekly expenditure. In any case, it would soon have run its course, and Brian was its only possible replacement. "D'you promise you'll find a way?" she said.

"To what?"

It was clear, even to the gullible Miss Hawkins, that Brian found the whole matrimonial prospect faintly resistible. "To marrying me," she said, wearily brazen.

"Of course I promise," he said. "We'll find a way. Don't you worry."

"Where will we live?" she said, then before he could answer, "I'd like you to move in here. But we'll need a bit more furniture."

What the hell? he thought, he might as well play her along totally. "That'll be very cosy," he said. "And when your tin-ship comes home, we'll re-furnish completely." By then he would be safely installed on Violet's velvet cushions well out of the Hawkins' reach or pleading. He was filled with utter contempt for her measly provincialism, and he stretched over and pocketed the last silver pile. "Till next Monday, then," he said, getting up.

"Perhaps you'll have news for me then," she said.

"Nothing's going to happen in a week," he said. "But don't you worry. I'll think of something."

His assurances should have appeased her, but somehow her anxieties remained. It wasn't that she didn't believe him. She was sure that he would do his best to find some solution, but there was no doubt that his mother was a formidable obstacle. They could only wait for her to die. She wished suddenly that she seriously believed in God so that she could offer a sincere prayer for Mrs. Watts's painless passing, bearing in mind that if she hung about much longer it would be at the cost of two people's happiness, and in God's reputed fairness, He would be judge. She saw Brian to the door, and stood there looking after him up the street. In her worried weariness, even the ticking appetite had deserted her, and it was a full five minutes before she left the porch and returned to the kitchen.

The diary lay on the table. She was faintly surprised that it was still locked. Had it been lying open it would have been almost as she expected. Her life had taken on such a pervading unreality that she no longer felt herself personally responsible for any turn of events. She looked around her denuded home and could not accept that she herself had stripped it. For a brief moment she recalled her pre-Brian days, when her nest-egg hatched cosily in the bank, when her accrued possessions hugged her like a womb, when the green book was locked and order-less. She looked back on those days with longing, and she wondered how, and on whose behalf, such confusion had invaded her nest. She tried to concentrate on her Monday pleasures, trying to see in them fair compensation for her loss. But now they appeared to her wasteful, disgusting even, and obscene, and she remembered Matron's terrible prophecy. She had been right. She was indeed a fallen and penniless woman. At the thought of Matron, and especially at the thought that she had proved so exact, Miss Hawkins rushed to the sitting-room, reaching automatically for her knitting, then freezing with fear as she recalled that it was no longer there. That disappearance too was an unreality outside her own making, and it left her defenceless and unarmed against the searing memories of her childhood. She was loathe to look for the scarf. She feared that, even if she found it, she could not accommodate the shape or texture it might have assumed. The scarf had colonized her almost as tyrannously as the diary, and her need for them both was equally obsessive. She could not bear to be in the house any longer. She needed the proximity of another human being, she needed to partake of some human enterprise, to reassure herself of the existence of a certain reality, and that given a chance, she would recognize it. She rushed to the wardrobe for her coat. And there, swinging its overburdened length from the skeleton hanger, hung the scarf, its needles upturned in one of her shoes. And in its hanging shadow, she saw Morris. She was not frightened, for after all, that was what the scarf was all about, a multi-coloured winding-sheet for an unburied grief. It was right and proper that Morris had appeared for a fitting. What did frighten her, though, was a total non-recollection of putting it there. Why on earth should she change its normal resting-place? It had taken itself there, she was sure. It had hung itself snugly next to her coat, as if it had in mind to go somewhere, to seek and find some target for its accumulated rainbow spleen. She smiled, not knowing why, or understanding the sudden stab of pleasure its discovery had given her. Tenderly she took it down from its hanger and folded it, admiring its proud, enduring length. It crossed her mind to cast off the stitches and hope that her occasional anger would subsequently abate. But she needed it, only a little longer, she thought, until Brian would take her hand and give her peace.

FAVOURS

She took the coloured folds and gently placed them in the bottom of her large shopping basket. Thenceforward the scarf would accompany her everywhere. Before leaving the house, she looked again in her diary. She was free of orders for the rest of the day, having already dutifully acquitted herself. She flicked through the remaining years' pages. And though she felt it was against all the rules to anticipate the future with any certainty, she turned the pages to her expected day of release. Just barely two months to go. She picked a small African violet that grew from a plant on the kitchen window-sill. Very gently she pressed it onto the page. By the time her sentence ended, it would be dry and filigree-aged, a fitting farewell to her green-leathered bondage. As she was closing the book she caught sight of the day of her freedom. It was Easter Monday.

16

EVERY SUBSEQUENT MONDAY MISS HAWKINS WAS TEMPTED TO play her last alarming card. But the little green book withheld the order. Besides she did not have the necessary service charge, but she feared that one day the diary would prescribe the offering and she would not have the wherewithal to obey. It was as well to be prepared. She looked about her. The only object left in the flat that could possibly fetch the required amount was the settee. To dispossess herself of that time-honoured accoutrement of service would be a major undertaking. And if she sold it, what then would serve as the altar for her supreme sacrifice? She knew it would have to be the bed, with Maurice tucked for shame underneath, but since that would be its future setting, she might as well get used to it. The location bothered her far less than the deed itself, and far less than its actual cost. She pictured her shy unmarried self in the attitude of wilful surrender, and recalling Matron's promise of the purgatorial fire, she shuddered. She tried to attach less value to that gift on which all her life she had kept such a tight hold. In Matron's terms she was already a fallen woman. For years now she had indulged her filthy pleasures, and sullied them further by payment. What difference now if she merely extended the range of her desire? So she tried to belittle herself, to rate as trash the last remnant of her virtue, but with all her reasoning, she could not deny its worth. If she hung on to it, it might not give her entry into heaven, but it would certainly help to save her from the fire. But then she thought Brian was sure to marry her, and no one need ever know that the loss of her virtue was premature. God wasn't that clever. For a long time she weighed in her mind the advantages and disadvantages of the diary's possible order, and in the process of her considerations, she grew more and more excited, and she regarded that as a sin, too, and knew that no matter what she did, she was irretrievably damned. There no longer seemed to be any point in limitations.

She went to the kitchen and unlocked her diary. She flicked through the pages. Her release was barely three weeks hence, and the African violet had already wept its bondage dry. The proximity of the date frightened her. She had so much to achieve in so short a time. She turned the pages back to the day's date. And boldly she wrote, "Sold the Settee."

She wrote out a little notice giving its description, and taking care to state the required price of £50. She took it straightway to the news-agent's and returned quickly in order to make full use of her last solid possession while there was still time. But first she took Maurice off the wall and leaned him in the corner of the settee. Then she snuggled up beside him. "Maurice," she said, "only another few weeks to my wedding." She looked up at him and had to adjust herself so that he could see her and hear her properly. And when he did, she thought he looked at her disbelievingly. "It's true," she said angrily. "You just wait and see." Now he looked angry, too, and he began to get on her nerves with his lack of enthusiasm. She was going to tell him about the settee and why she was selling it, but she didn't think he deserved her confidence. But she had to tell someone. She had to air the terrible words, as if by confession, the deed itself would absolve her. "He'll *have* to marry me, Maurice," she said defiantly. "You know why, don't you? It's because I'm going to . . ." She stopped, choking on the blasphemous words. "Well, you know what I mean," she said.

He looked at her, his moustache drooping. She wanted to bash his face in. She turned her back on him and sulked into the cushion. She couldn't bear Maurice's disapproval. She ought never to have told him. He had been deeply disappointed in her. She turned round quickly. "I was only joking," she said, and she saw him smile with relief. At the time she meant it. She, Miss Jean Hawkins, would remain a maiden until her wedding night, but during Brian's service she would assume the role of someone else, an act of sacrifice that was not hers, but performed on behalf of another whom she would gladly consign to the fire. She would be proxy for Matron, she decided, and whether she was dead or alive, God would take careful note, and kindle the flame. It would be a joy to attend such a service. She was delighted with her new-found solution, and she leaned towards Maurice and embraced him. "Can't take a joke, can you?" she said.

The following day, while she was polishing what little furniture was left in her flat, the bell rang. She took off her apron and answered the door.

"You have a settee for sale," the man said.

She started. She had forgotten her little notice. She hadn't slept most of the night and now she recollected what had been nagging her. "Yes," she said hopelessly. "Come in."

He followed her into the sitting-room. He loosened his scarf, and she saw with gathering dismay that by his collar he was a priest of sorts, and she was tempted to grasp his sleeve and beg absolution. How could she take money from a man of God in order to buy herself a sure ticket to hell? She wanted to tell him that the settee was not for sale, that she'd changed her mind, but he was already appraising it, fingering the moquette, caressing it as if it pleased him well. "We're building a little community centre," he said, "for the old people, you know. We need a lot of comfortable chairs. There's no better way to serve our Lord than in the care of the old and lonely."

Oh, my God, she thought, if only he knew to what iniquities that settee had been witness, in what heathen delights it had played such a pleasured role. She almost begged him not to touch it.

"I like it," he said with a happy, unbearable innocence, "but it's a little more than the kitty can afford. Can you sell it a little cheaper?"

She wanted to give it to him, as a way of cleansing herself, as an atonement, but such largesse was impracticable for one only bent on further trespass. "I need fifty pounds," she said simply.

He looked at the fireside chair. "Are you thinking of selling that, too?" he said.

It would leave her with nowhere at all to sit, but her scarf no longer needed that resting-place, and she was happy to throw it in for nothing.

"That's very kind of you," the cloth said.

She looked round frantically for anything else that would help furnish his centre. "Is there anything else you want?" she said.

"Are you moving?" he said, noting the over-all bareness of the room. "Yes," she said brightly, "I'm getting married. We're moving to the country."

"Congratulations," he said. "That's happy news." And almost in the same breath, "Are you taking your dining-table with you?"

"No, you can have that, too," she said. "It'll come in handy for the old people." God must surely be listening, she thought, and taking note and marking up her credits.

"You're much too kind," he said.

"It's to celebrate my wedding," she laughed, thinking that Maurice and she would henceforth have to eat off the floor.

He paid her £50 in crisp £5 notes, saying that he would send a van in the afternoon. He blessed her for her kindness and wished her well in her marriage. Miss Hawkins felt little scruple in having hoodwinked him. She had, after all, given him more or less what was left of her home. She decided that in the evening she and Maurice would have a last supper together. In three days Brian would come, and during that time, she would prepare Matron for her eternal damnation.

On Monday morning, Miss Hawkins woke up screaming. In her dream, there had been no location, no people and no sign of life or habitation. Just sound. The sound of bells that had begun as a gentle tinkle, almost inaudible. She'd strained her ears, and in response, the volume increased and assumed a hint of a melody which she half recognized as wedding chimes. She smiled and listened, urging them with her humming, until they pealed out, piercing the bright void with their nuptial message. Unmistakable. She lay back and listened, as the whole invisible world tolled her free-dom. The morning would bring her wedding-day, not in the Law's mind perhaps, but certainly in Brian's and her own. His service to her would conscript him into matrimony, and the bells rang out their sanction. And rang and rang, faster and louder, and so fast and so loud that the melody stumbled as the speed and volume overtook it in a cacophonous and deafening din. Her head had be-come the bell-tower of a great cathedral, and the noise pierced her ear-drums, and she awoke screaming with the stab of pain. She got up quickly. She wished she could miss out on this day, that some proxy would swallow it on her behalf, that the next morning she could wake and survey the ruins or otherwise of her aching hopes. Knowing what she had to do, and knowing too that there was no alternative, deeply depressed her, and wandering through her bare and desolate home did little to raise her hopes. There's nothing for it, she thought, there's no longer anything to lose. The final humilia-tion, if such it turned out to be, would belong to Matron. With this thought she steeled herself to dressing and making breakfast. She would need all her strength for this day. When she had eaten, she set about to clean the flat. In its denuded state, it did not take her very long. She spent most of the time in her bedroom, changing the linen and covering her shameful stratagem with her best counterpane. She wondered whether she should turn the bed down. She considered that that was part of the service, and Brian's department. She would be glad to leave it to him. She could contribute nothing more. She would pay the price, shut her eyes tightly, invoke Matron and unlock her sen-sible legs. She shut the door quickly behind her. For some reason she could not bear to stay in the room.

In the kitchen the diary lay open with seven full pages to her freedom. Its current blank page called her attention. Somehow an order must be prescribed. To delay it, she flicked through the years of good conduct and obedience and she experienced a small plea-sure of achievement. If she could acquit herself as well in the re-maining days of her sentence she would have gained a small victory, even if everything else around her had crumbled in its name. The thought cheered her a little and gave her sufficient courage to pick up her pen and consider the day's terrible order. It wasn't that she was wanting in the courage to prescribe it, rather that she was lacking in words. As a literary exercise, her diary was a monument to purity unsmudged by a single unsavoury word. She couldn't imagine that there was a clean expression for what she was about to do, and she could not sully her diary with its description. After a little thought she wrote, "Spent £50." The diary would understand what she was trying to say. As she read it over, she realized that there were loopholes in the order. It could have meant the expenditure of £50 on anything or in any place. Miss Hawkins had always been very strict with herself, so she added specifics to the original order so that it finally read, "Spent £50 on Brian's service, and on one single item." That order was air-tight, with no loophole for escape or misinterpretation. She read it over. It was written down once and for all, and it was now inescapable.

She wondered whether she should bother to make a sponge. It would be the first Monday for many years that she had by-passed this leaden trimming of the ceremony. But there was no longer anywhere comfortable to take tea, or any surface to bear the candle-light, or any altar to curtain from the daylight. No, she decided, to-day there would be no ceremony. It would be a simple service, shrineless, and without cake, but God was everywhere and He could be wooed direct, without the trappings of ritual. So having decided against making a cake, and having made out the order, there was nothing for her to do until Brian came. She wanted to go into her bedroom to fetch a handkerchief, but she was afraid to enter the room lest the sight of the clean sheets and their avowed purpose would shake her firm intent. For now there was no turning back. It was indelibly written.

She sat on the floor of the sitting-room and tried not to think of what the afternoon would bring. But it was difficult not to think about it. In that empty room there was no solid object on which to focus her attention, and all her slippery day-dreams led to the white-sheeted shrine. She concentrated on Matron, and hoped that her hatred would freeze her image long enough to endure the service. She had no idea of how long it would take, but she hoped it would be quick and easily forgettable, and she could tick it off in her little book, and when no-one was looking, she could transfer the same order to her wedding day, where it would find proper and legal timing. She thought of Matron, and for once could not hold on to that reliable irritant, and she feared that her dark shadow would lurk somewhere else that afternoon, out of her desperate reach. She feared that her intended proxy would not materialize, and it would be she, Miss Jean Hawkins, and no other who would taint those sheets and who would cry out to God for mercy, pleading that she was only obeying orders. She decided that she would straightway put on her wedding-dress, just to satisfy herself in her own mind that she was a bride and that the sheets were her God-given entitlement.

Slowly she entered the bedroom and laid the bridal gown on the bed. As she dressed, she felt the need for some music, and she switched on the radio to the morning service. She was glad the organ was playing. For the first time in many years she thought of her mother, and she had a sudden longing to have known her. She was pretty certain, and Matron had lost no opportunity to confirm it, that her mother had never worn such a dress, but had doubtless day-dreamed herself into the white and pure veil. She looked upon her own prospective marriage as a vindication of the unjustness of her mother's life, and a chance to give the lie to Matron's calumny.

When she was dressed, she drew the veil over her head and walked slowly around the flat to the organ's mournful tune. In such a way she spent what was left of the morning, acclimatizing herself to her new status, and in doing so validating in advance the events of the afternoon. And so vivid and real was her marital status that by the end of the morning she was eager to claim her conjugal rights, and almost resented that she had to pay for them.

She took off the dress and hung it beneath its cellophane cover. Already she had ideas of having it altered now that it had served its original purpose, of cutting it down to serve as a cocktail dress for the dinner-dances that Brian would take her to. The tiara and veil she would keep as a souvenir to ensure her of a passport to heaven.

She was too excited to eat any lunch. She straightened the counterpane where the tiara had left its print. In her excitement, she'd forgotten to set out the service charge. She took the vicar's wad of bills and placed them on the table next to the lamp. She wished they weren't so clean. As her final preparation she took Maurice off the wall and wondered where to put him. She couldn't put him under the bed, for that was his punishment place and he had done no wrong. But she had lied to him and was about to cheat him, and he had to be well out of the way of her deception. She would put him in the kitchen. In the pantry against the wall. Afterwards she would try to explain to him. She might even tell him the truth, and risk his desertion as well. In any case, she would soon be a respectable married woman, and perhaps she ought to think of giving Maurice his marching orders. She placed him gently on the floor, facing the wall. "We'll talk it all over this evening," she said.

The door-bell rang and in the instant splintered all her morning illusions. Now the reality of the afternoon's programme could no longer and in no way be disguised. Her knees sank to the cold pantry floor, and she prayed to God to forgive her.

At the sight of the bunch of flowers in his hand, she took heart, and knew that, whatever the price, all would be well. He, for his part, mindful that this was his last Hawkins call, was prepared to court and to promise and to offer her his all. He followed her into the sitting-room. He was shocked by its bare appearance, but he was careful not to comment. Whatever excuse she made, it was clear that poverty was overwhelming her.

"I'm buying new furniture," she said, hugging the flowers, and regretting that there was no table to put them on. "I got so tired of the old stuff. In any case," she prattled on, "if you're to start a new life, you need new things to go with it." She giggled, almost crushing her bouquet in a hot spasm of embarrassment.

For a moment he felt ashamed, but finding such an emotion so inconvenient to accommodate, he changed it easily and quickly into anger. He could have hit her for being so gullible.

"Did you think about your mother?" she said.

"Yes. I'll find a solution, don't you worry. You're right. We should be together, you and I," he said.

Her heart leapt with gratitude, and she crushed the flower stems so hard that the sap seeped through her fingers. "Oh, Brian," was all she could say, and he winced at the whine in the name. But it wasn't the name, he assured himself. Miss Hawkins would have whined Felix, too. "Well," he said, business-like, "where are we going to trade this afternoon?" As he said it, he realized that the brave little Miss Hawkins was finally going to sample the deep end, and that the leaden sponge and sickly port were probably on the bedside table. She looked up at him shyly and confirmed his thoughts.

"Follow me," she said. Her voice came out as a plaintive squeak and he walked behind her and noticed that every part of her poor unyielding body was a-tremble. For a moment he thought he might refuse, as a last single act of decency. But what the hell, £50 was £50, and it could go towards the honeymoon. He decided instead that he would be extra gentle with her and that he would give of his best. All she would ever have of him was a memory. The least he could do was to make sure that it was beautiful.

And that he honestly intended, and perhaps it was not his fault that the legacy he bequeathed her proved otherwise. She lay in the semi-darkness, with her eyes screw-tight closed, trying with all her strength to enlist even the shadow of Matron into her shame. She wept with the fear and failure of it all, and prayed that the dear and gentle Maurice, with his ears to the pantry wall, did not hear her cry of pain.

"Why don't you put your flowers in water?" he said when they returned to the sitting-room. She hadn't recalled dropping them, but they were strewn over the floor. She hadn't the strength to bend and pick them up.

"I'll gather them for you," he said. He put them back into a bunch and re-presented them. "To my future wife," he said.

"Oh, Brian."

He tried not to hear it, but pressed on. "Would you mind if my mother lived with us?" he said. "It's the only solution."

"She'd be very welcome," Miss Hawkins said, not daring to accept what was meant by it all.

"Then I'm proposing," he said. He waited for the "Oh, Brian," and when it was out, he took her hand. "We'll be married after Easter," he said.

She opened her mouth and he put his fingers gently on her lips. He simply couldn't bear to hear that whine again. "I'll see you next Monday," he said, "and we can make all the arrangements."

"Mrs. Jean Watts," she squeaked. "Oh, Brian, I can't believe it."

"You will," he said. "You might even live to regret it."

"Never," she said.

He put his arm round her, leading her to the front door. "Now you start making a list of all the things we shall need for the wedding. I'll pay for everything," he said.

She was so overwhelmed with happiness that she couldn't even bring out an "Oh, Brian." It was there in her cheeks, but she had to swallow it to stop herself from crying.

"Till next Monday, then, Miss Hawkins," he laughed. "Shan't be using that much longer, shall we."

She watched him down the street, and he, turning, looked back at her. He gave her his widest smile. He could afford to after all, in the comforting knowledge that he would never set eyes on her again.

Miss Hawkins returned to the kitchen. She walked very slowly, partly because of the unaccustomed stirrings in her body, and partly because her sudden joy had almost immobilized her. She sat down on her last remaining kitchen chair and unlocked her diary. She opened it at the current page and read the order aloud. Its execution had been the most masterful achievement to date. Before ticking it, she enclosed it in a red-crayoned flower-frame, and then very slowly, and with both trembling hands, she set her crimson seal. She savoured the mark for a long moment. She knew that henceforward till the end of her sentence the orders would be simple errands of joy. Brian was going to marry her, and God would understand her frailty and bless their union.

She locked the little book and took Maurice out of the pantry. She stood him on the kitchen work-table opposite her chair. "We're getting married after Easter, Maurice," she said. He was smiling, happy for her. She felt she owed him some kind of apology. "I had to do it, Maurice," she said, "just to make sure of him. But it wasn't very nice. Honestly," she pleaded. "It was really quite awful." He commiserated with her, full of understanding. Gently she put him back on the sitting-room wall. She wondered what she would do with him when she was married. She couldn't send him away after all the support he had given her. Perhaps she could introduce him to Brian's mother, though she did not think they would have much in common. Perhaps she would keep him a secret in the pantry. He would be someone to talk to when old Mrs. Watts started to get on her nerves. She was determined, however, to make the old woman comfortable, for Brian's sake. She had to decide where to accommodate her. The spare room that she had set aside for Brian's occasional need for privacy must now be given over to his mother. She would furnish it as a bed-sitting-room, with a little gas-ring, so that she need never leave it and her incontinence would at least be space-contained. Once a week she would give it a good clean-out, and Mrs. Watts could meanwhile sit in the hall. Until the old woman died, Brian would have to share her bedroom. She wondered whether what had taken place that afternoon would be a regular feature of their marriage. She rather hoped that once was enough, that it was a declaration so graphic that it need not be re-confirmed. If Brian, however, did insist on such a right, she would grit her teeth and take comfort in the fact that at least she was not paying for her pain.

She went into the bedroom to remove the evidence of her innocent blackmail. She opened up the bed and saw the blood on the sheet. Quickly she covered it so that God would not see. Then she sat on the bed and recalled with neither anger nor fear the small smudge of womanhood on the bathroom lino all those years ago. From the naked bulb poor Morris choked on her painful protest, but even that swinging shadow was now still. Perhaps at last she had trapped that restless grief and she could call an end to all her mourning. She felt strangely at peace. Somehow, in her mind, the blood on the sheet seemed to be a proof that Matron had been there after all.

17

MRS. WATTS WOKE UP ON EASTER MONDAY MORNING AND THROUGH half shut eyes, peered at her new bonnet hanging on the brass rail at the foot of the bed. The sight of it informed her of the auspicious day and the events of that day, and she stirred with excitement. It was the first new hat she'd had in many years. Brian had given it to her for his wedding. And that took place this afternoon in a smart hotel in the country with a woman whose name she had forgotten, and who, for some unknown reason, called her son Felix. She got out of bed and went quickly to her bathroom. She had not had a single accident since her residency at The Petunias. Mrs. Watts was now continent. Whether it was the plush carpeting that restrained her, or the pretty sheets on the bed, she did not stop to question. Perhaps it was simply a matter of constant and friendly care and attention. Whatever the reason, you could take Mrs. Watts anywhere.

A few miles away the nearly Mrs. Watts was checking on her "something borrowed, something blue." A friend had lent her a beaded handbag, and she'd bought a small piece of blue ribbon that she tied, garter-like, round her thigh. Violet Makins was a superstitious woman, and though she had no doubt about the rightness of her marriage with Felix Watts, she was taking no chances. Her horoscope had pointed to Easter Monday as an auspicious date for their union: Some weeks before she had attended a séance, and dear George had materialized to wish her well, and to advise a wedding-breakfast in his old country club in Berkshire. This she had arranged, together with a honeymoon in Casablanca which was prompted not by the stars but by her cousin's availability list. No matter. Her clairvoyant had prophesied a tropical holiday, so all in all the astral influence had been fully respected. She took out her manicure box and set to polishing her nails.

Another few miles away, and in a different direction, Brian Watts, twice-promised groom, sneaked out of his house carrying a large hold-all. In his pin-striped suit and pointed shoes, he looked like a travelling salesman with a suit-case full of cunning. Unlike his mother before him, he stopped in the street, put down his case and looked back at the house in which he'd lived for over fifty years. He saw the dingy net curtains and the squalid, peeling paintwork, and he wondered how he'd lived there for so long. He hailed a taxi at the corner of the street, and once inside, he pinned a white carnation in his button-hole.

Not far away, Miss never-to-be-Mrs. Watts was making the biggest and richest sponge cake of her culinary career. She loaded it into the oven and went back to her pile of pillows on the sitting-room floor. Between sips of port, she flicked through the holiday brochures she had gathered in armfuls at the travel agency. For a long time she studied each handout, weighing the comparative lures of the Riviera and the Adriatic and the more expensive Atlantic. She couldn't help feeling that they all looked the same. But Spain looked extra romantic with its hotels right on the beaches, and dancing by moonlight on fairy-lit terraces. She would try to persuade Brian to a Spanish honeymoon. She looked up at Maurice on the wall. She knew she must take him down soon because Brian was expected within the hour, yet more and more she was reluctant to part with him. His disposal seemed always to be a prelude to some move of deception, and even now, when the future seemed plain sailing, she wasn't quite convinced that her powers of guile and persuasion, such as they were, would not be called upon again. Maurice had become a kind of moral straitjacket, that, when discarded, left her prey to all manner of immodest temptation. "I wish you could come to Spain with us, Maurice," she said. He wasn't looking at her and his expression was inscrutable. She took it as disapproval and was annoyed at this right he'd assumed to judge her behaviour. In one area of her consciousness she knew that one clean swipe with a wet sponge would obliterate Maurice once and for all, but over the years she had renewed and revitalized that moustache as if it bristled from a pad of warm and human flesh, and to wipe him clean would have been tantamount to murder. On the other hand, she really did not know how to accommodate him after her marriage. He was essentially a private companion, and therefore unshareable. She could not imagine that in her future life she would need a great deal of privacy. Such a need, she thought, would reflect poorly on their union. In any case, privacy required space, and what with Brian and his old mother-lodger, there would be little of that. The problem of how to accommodate Maurice seemed to her insuperable, and all she could do was delay the decision until she came back from her honeymoon. Meanwhile, she would put him in the pantry.

She got up to take him off the wall and sniffed an ominous smell from the kitchen. She had forgotten to take out the sponge. She rushed to open the oven door, and through the smoke she discerned a charred platform with something of an apron stage jutting over the rim of the mould. She pulled it out with a hasty oven-glove and her eyes smarted from the smoke. Then turned to tears with the realization that on this, of all days, she could offer Brian no delicacy. And if Brian had been coming, he would most certainly have thanked her for it. She regarded the burnt offering as a terrible foreboding and she blamed Maurice and all the deliberations about his future that had so detained her. Angrily she went back to the sitting-room and unhooked him from the wall. Now she would put him under the bed because she had to punish him. She forbore to look at him as she carried him into the bedroom. Then she opened all the windows in the flat in an attempt to get rid of the smell of burning.

It was almost three o'clock and Brian was always punctual. She made a neat pile of the brochures in the sitting-room, putting the

Spanish folder on the top. Then she sat on the floor and waited. In the silence of her echoless sitting-room, she listened for footsteps on the pavement outside. It was holiday time, so there was less than the usual activity in the street. People had gone to the seaside or the fairs, and for the first time in her life, she thought about other people's pleasures without envy. Soon all the fairs in the world would be hers, and every inch of sandy beach. She wished the street well of its bank holiday and gave a small but undisturbed thought as to why Brian was late. He was probably walking, she thought, since buses were few and far between, and to pass the time, she shadowed him from his terraced house in Romilly Road, past the closed shops in the High Street, generously timing his waiting at kerbs for the occasional car to pass, until he reached the corner of her street. Then he stopped, perhaps to look at his watch, and he would note that he was late and he would quicken his stride to his bride-to-be. She listened for his hurried footsteps, and all she heard was a distant church bell. She was afraid to look at her watch, for the seeds of panic were undeniably sprouting. She wished she had Maurice to talk to. She thought she might retrieve him for a while, but there would be no time. Brian was bound to come shortly. They had so much to discuss and so many arrangements to make. Idly she opened the Spanish folder, and as she did so, she could not help but look at her watch and register the time. Ten minutes to four. Quite irrelevantly she wished that her room was furnished as before so that she could rise from one chair and agitatedly move across the room to another. But now surrounded by all that bareness, there was no punctuation to her fear, no resting-place for her mounting panic, and she froze in her squat on the floor and tried not to think that he had jilted her. She scratched in her mind for some excuse on his behalf, and decided that his mother, through illness or sheer blood-mindedness, had delayed him. She began to hate her, and fear her future role as daughter-in-law. But it was a role that she had to envisage else face the outrageous reality of a life in ruins. She would put Brian's mother in her place, she thought. She would let her know in no uncertain terms that any part of the flat outside the spare room was strictly out of bounds. That once a week she could have a bath and once a week she could sit diapered in the hall while her room was being cleaned. Brian would arrive any moment now, full of apologies and begging her understanding. She would withhold it for a while, then gradually give in, and they would get down to the arrangements for their future. Perhaps, in view of the sponge-cake fiasco, he might even offer to take her out to tea, for there would be no time for servicing this afternoon. In any case, she could no longer afford it.

She got up from the floor and crossed the room to the front window. She drew back the net curtains which she knew was a very vulgar thing to do, for it indicated an unhealthy interest in other people's business. But she felt justified, since it was her business, her very own, that she was investigating. It was in fact a life or death investigation and a single footfall in that shattering holiday silence could tip the scales. She noticed a woman in the window of the house opposite, engaged in exactly the same pursuit, and she wondered as to the comparative urgency of her search. On seeing Miss Hawkins, the woman dropped her curtain, ashamed to be discovered in such idleness and curiosity, humiliated by the screaming loneliness she may have betrayed. But Miss Hawkins did not lower her curtain. The lonelinesss and fear behind her net had, at that moment, far less priority in her thoughts than the possibility of deliverance from outside. If that deliverance did not come, even tardily, she would turn her back on the street and there would be ample time and tears to flood the ruins of her hope.

She stood at the window for a long time. Once she heard footsteps, but even with her optimism, she had to dismiss them as the skipping steps of a child. She hoped it would not skip by her door, for she feared she might have gone out and done it harm. She forced herself to look at her watch. Four-thirty. She would not give way to sorrow or mourning, for that would have pronounced finality. Instead, she battened onto anger and held on to it fast, refusing recourse to her knitting, which would have tempered it and weaned it altogether. She needed her anger now as never before. She needed to cling to an infinite fury, for any alternative now was a show of abdication. She turned from the window and she screamed long and silently into the empty room, knowing that Maurice, from his punishment pen under the bed, would, like a dog, hear that cry of pain that lay far beyond the reaches of the human ear.

She rushed to her diary. She was determined to hold on to her hope, yet what she wrote down on the current page indicated a small act of surrender. "Went to Brian's and got all my money back," she saw that she had written, and she noticed that her handwriting was unusually untidy. The diary had ordered it, she thought. It had nothing to do with her. Her wise diary was simply being sensible, ensuring at least a future roof over her head, even if it sheltered an unbearable and aching void. She put on her coat, grabbed her large shopping-bag, irritated by its commodious bulk but feeling the need for the scarf's protection as an escape-route for her spleen. She was going to go straight to Brian's house, and if he wasn't in, she would go to his mother and tell on him.

She had to walk all the way since there was no transport, but her anger did not abate. In fact, it accrued with each wearisome step, and by the time she reached her mother-in-law's house, she was seething with a weary rage. There were three door-bells and she rang them all. When there was no immediate reply she leaned against them, listening to their triple echo. And when the front door opened, she flung her wrath at the poor unfortunate woman who had bewilderedly answered the emergency holiday call.

"Brian Watts," Miss Hawkins shouted as a summons.

A small look of suspicious recognition passed between the two women. Each knew they had seen the other before, but Miss Hawkins had neither time nor inclination to enquire where they had met.

"You were at my dad's funeral," the woman said. She had recalled Miss Hawkins as a gate-crasher, and her manner was by no means friendly.

"He's the middle bell and he's out," she said.

"How d'you know he's out?"

" 'Cos he hasn't answered his bell, has he?" she said insolently. "You've rung it hard enough."

"I want to see his mother then," Miss Hawkins demanded, as if the poor woman were Mrs. Watts's keeper.

"She doesn't live here any more."

"Where has she gone?" Miss Hawkins' voice had suddenly lost

its tone of command. With Mrs. Watts's disappearance, she had an instinctive feeling that she was going to need this woman as a source of information. She must be polite.

"She's in an old age home. The Petunias. Hoity-toity."

"Do you have the address?" Miss Hawkins said, and added, "please," plaintively, knowing that her arrogant manner hitherto hadn't merited the woman's co-operation.

"Just a minute," she said. She left the door and disappeared into a room off the hall.

Miss Hawkins had time to consider this latest piece of information, and she certainly did not warm to its deceptive implications. The woman came back to the door with a small white card. She handed it over. Miss Hawkins didn't want to bother her further, but there was one question that needed to be asked. She was so afraid for its answer that she hesitated, and the woman was already closing the door.

"How long has she been in the home?" Miss Hawkins panted through the crack.

"Must be three months now," the woman said. "She moved out on New Year's Day." Then the crack closed. From that side of the door at least, there was nothing more to say.

Miss Hawkins grabbed at the scarf in her shopping-bag as some contact for comfort. She couldn't understand why Brian had lied to her, but she dared not allow herself to connect it with his non-appearance that afternoon. He would have an explanation, she was sure. He must have arrived while she was out, was probably even now waiting on her door-step or perhaps he had left a note explaining his late call. She had to get back home immediately. In the distance she was relieved to see a lone bus travelling down the High Street. She ran as fast as her shopping-bag would allow and she reached the stop in good time. On the slow ride home, she convinced herself that Brian or a note would be waiting for her, and it would explain everything. She now regretted that she had trusted him so little and had left the house with no-one to wait for him. That was no way to be a good and loving wife, she told herself, and she would beg Brian to forgive her for her mistrust. She wished the bus would hurry. There was very little traffic about and no need for extra caution, yet it dawdled at every stop- and traffic-light and finally announced an all-change at the library. The wheel had come full circle, and Miss Hawkins regarded it as a fitting terminus and a good sign that all would be well. Now she hurried down the maze of side-streets, short-cutting to her home, primping her hair with her free hand so that she would look well for her groom. She hadn't given another thought to his mother since leaving his house, but now as she turned the corner of her street, his gross deception suddenly grazed her heart and her anger returned. There was no Brian waiting at the door, and as she turned to open the gate, she caught sight of the woman across the street dropping her net curtain. Miss Hawkins levelled with her veiled, steady stare, and stuck her tongue out as far as it would go.

She unlocked her front door, but there was no note in the letter-box. Beside it she off-loaded her shopping-bag, prepared for another sortie, for she knew she would not stay in her empty flat and wait for him much longer. She looked at her watch. Six o'clock. It seemed to her now that there was little reason in hoping any longer. At this thought she began to tremble. She went into her sitting-room and stood rigid in its emptiness, trying to control the convulsions of her body. She thought she might be having a fit, but she was afraid to lie down for fear of not being able to rise again. She clutched the knob of the sitting-room door. She was sweating, yet she was cold. She was quivering, yet she was not afraid. All she knew was hate and anger, and a bruised and harrowed heart. She saw that her grip on the door-handle was so tight that her knuckles were white with strain. A small dribble of spit oozed over her chin. She had a strange and hysterical notion that her body was leaking its fury. And for the first time she gave way to fear. And that fear loosened her white grip on the door-knob and bullied her into the kitchen to face the first unobeyed order of her long sentence. The red tick was unachievable, and for the dutiful Miss Hawkins, it was the final deprivation. With a small and desperate scream, she drew an angry line through the ill-written order. She had never written it. It had never been there. She hadn't meant to get her money back. Ever. It was something different she'd had in mind. Something very different indeed. And she wrote it boldly, in large capitals.

The four-letter word dropped from her pen as naturally as blood from a wound. For she had to bleed somehow, for her injury was deep and infinitely painful. As she dropped the pen from her hand, she dribbled once more her spleen, and her blood-shot eyes recorded what her diary had ordered. "KILL." She picked up her shopping-bag and fled from the house.

She'd picked up two weeks of her pension money in advance. The post office always made that concession prior to bank holidays. It was her minimal housekeeping money, but for some reason she felt she would not need it. She would take her turbulent rage to The Petunias by taxi.

She found one cruising at the corner of her street. She tried to sit back comfortably on the upholstered seat as the written instructions suggested. She had, after all, not sat in a comfortable chair in many weeks. She was very unused to taxis, and in any case, her stumbling rage would not allow her to relax, and she sat stiffly on the edge of her seat, wiping the endless spittle from her chin and in her cold sweat, looking out of the window but seeing nothing. Unlike the bus the taxi was speeding, and tuned harmoniously with her growing rage. By the time they reached The Petunias' drive, she was once more a-tremble in each part of her body, and when she stepped from the taxi she tried to steady herself, but her body quivered like a lately rooted arrow. She shuddered up the drive.

A gardener was weeding one of the border flower-beds, and as she approached, she shouted, "Mrs. Watts?" She didn't want to stop. She hoped his answer would come in her transit.

"Over in the annexe," he called to her without looking up from his hoe, and he waved an arm in the direction of a separate building on the side of the main house. So with no interruption of her clenched footsteps, she made her way across the lawns.

The door to the annexe was open, but there was no-one about. Without stopping she called down the long corridor, "Mrs. Watts?" There was no response. She turned about and tried the other side of the rectangle, shouting her plaintive summons. This time a door opened and an old lady peered out, and seeing another human being and the prospect of some company, flung a large smile in her direction. She waited for Miss Hawkins to reach her door.

"Are you looking for somebody?" she said, though it was difficult to imagine that a visitor was bent on any other errand.

"Mrs. Watts," Miss Hawkins said, loud and clear.

"She's been out, I know," Miss Winters said. "I don't think she's back yet. I'll go and see. Would you like to wait in my room for a moment?"

Miss Hawkins was in no mood for pleasantries, but she could have done with a chair as some means of calming her taut and quivering nerves. And she had to stop her footsteps if only to wipe the dribble from her chin. She followed Miss Winters into her room and took the easy-chair that she offered.

"I'll just go and see if she's back," Miss Winters said. "Won't be a moment."

She wasn't a moment either, but it was long enough to give Miss Hawkins time to catch sight of a large framed photograph on the dressing-table, time enough to stir a strange and unnerving interest, time to investigate the small, pale, unhappy faces, time enough to curdle a sick flicker of recall. Then Miss Winters was back, standing in the doorway.

"You can wait here for her if you like," she said. She moved over to the bed and sat down.

Miss Hawkins stared at her. "What's your name?" she said.

"Miss Winters."

It rang no bell. She turned and looked again at the photograph. She wanted to be sick and she didn't know why. "Where's Mrs. Watts?" she said.

"Oh, she had a big day to-day. Went to her son's wedding. I was asked, but I'm not feeling too well. Brian is his name. A charming man."

The news did not register immediately, for Miss Hawkins was too concerned with the nightmare of the woman's identity. She looked again at the photograph, and picked it up to examine it closer. In the front row, she saw her pigtailed self, and next to her poor Morris in her unhanged pre-woman freedom.

"My little orphans," the woman on the bed was saying.

"Married?" Miss Hawkins said, very, very gently.

"Yes. A nice lady, too. Violet something or other. Mrs. Watts looked so smart in her new bonnet."

Very slowly Miss Hawkins took the scarf from out of her shopping-bag. She ran its serpentine length through her fingers, looking for a suitable colour that would translate her rising bile. Somewhere around the middle, she found a foot of olive green. It would do. Slowly she approached the bed as if to embrace her, and she placed the green against Matron's rigid and starched throat. Then she wound it round once, slowly and strongly, pulling tightly on each end, watching the old woman's bewildered stare, the bulging, tearful eyes, the jutting forehead vein, and at last the lolling tongue. How like poor Morris she looks, Miss Hawkins thought, and a strange calm invaded her. She pushed the dead woman back onto the pillows, and as she did so, Matron's arm knocked over the polythene-wrapped singing Mary, and a muffled, unseasonal, off-key "Silent Night" tinkled like a cracked, passing bell. Miss Hawkins stared long at the terrible face and the starched neck so full of scarf. She marvelled that out of all the yardage of her years' anger, out of the long, long distance of her shattered childhood, it had taken but six inches of olive green to wipe the jagged slate clean. From the ends of the stranglehold, Miss Hawkins picked up the knitting needles, and slowly and with infinite care, she cast off the stitches. She placed the empty needles one on each side of Matron's head, and the symmetry pleased her. Matron would have said that she was a good girl. Then she picked up her empty shopping-bag, and left for home.

In the kitchen she unlocked her diary and ticked off the final capital order with a small and secret joy. She noticed that the African violet had crumbled into a frail dry lace, as if freedom were too burdensome a bondage. She gathered up Maurice from under the bed and took him into the sitting-room. She sat on the floor and held him before her. "I am innocent, Maurice," she said. Then, holding him close, she sat and waited for them to come and look after her.